JOAN JOHNSTON

Winter Magic

A BITTER CREEK NOVELLA

This book is dedicated to my
critique group partners
Barbara Darling, Rohini Grace,
and Barbra Cohn.

Chapter 1

When you looked like a monster, you tended to avoid people. So when Mike Sullivan saw the dilapidated pickup stalled on the side of the road, he shuddered at the realization that he might have to stop his truck and help. Some poor soul had slid off the highway, likely as a result of the treacherous blizzard that had descended from the heavens an hour ago like a howling fury.

Mike slowed his Chevy and searched for a figure in the back window of an ancient Dodge pickup. He heaved a sigh of relief when he didn't see anyone in the fading daylight. Apparently, the driver had abandoned his precariously perched vehicle. Mike hoped whoever it was had gotten picked up. The thirty-below weather was merciless. It killed without caring.

As his headlights flashed on the snowdrifted side window of the blue Dodge, he hissed in a breath. "What the—" A woman and a child were huddled together in the front seat. Mike resisted the urge to hit the brakes, instead easing off the gas until his rusted-out Chevy slowed to a stop fifty feet beyond the other vehicle.

He swore under his breath. Ever since the brutal grizzly attack five years ago that had resulted in most of his face being torn off, he'd kept his distance from strangers. It had taken hundreds of stitches to put him back together, and after the black threads came out, he looked like a modern-day Frankenstein.

Mike hated his older brother for convincing him, "The scars aren't so bad." The lie had been exposed when he'd come home from the hospital and his five-year-old nephew had taken one look at him, yelped like a whipped dog, and scrambled away in fright.

Mike had moved out of the house where he'd grown up and into a small log home on the edge of Glacier National Park. He worked on the Rafter S, his family's cattle ranch, but otherwise kept to himself. He shopped in nearby Whitefish late at night to avoid being seen, because the scars on his face and neck and hands made kids shrink from him in fear and caused horrified grownups to look at him with pity.

Mike rearranged his black wool scarf to conceal the mutilation. The weather was excuse enough to be covered up. He pulled his felt Stetson low to hide his forehead so his guarded eyes were all anyone could see of his face.

He dreaded what he knew was coming, but he had no choice except to grit his teeth and bear it. When that woman and her child saw his face—what was left of his face—they might choose to stay where they were rather than come with him. But he couldn't leave them marooned in a gale-force blizzard. It was late enough in the day, and the snowstorm was fierce enough, that no one else was likely to come along before morning. The two of them could end up badly frostbitten, or even freeze to death, before they were found.

Making sure his scars were shielded, he backed his truck up until he was only a few feet in front of the stranded vehicle. He watched in the rearview mirror as the driver's-side door was shoved open. Because of the way the truck was tilted, Mike could see that the two of them were going to have a hard time making it safely to the ground. He took a deep breath, checked one last time to make sure that only his deep-set blue eyes were visible, and stepped down from his truck.

In several long strides, he reached the driver's-side door. The woman lost her balance stepping out of the tilted truck, and he caught her under the arms to keep her from falling. He felt her stiffen and let go the instant he was sure her feet were solidly on the ground.

She pivoted toward him, and he clamped his teeth to keep from gasping at the sight of her. Before he'd lost his looks, Mike had been a connoisseur of female beauty. He took in her vulnerable, sky-blue eyes, delicate brows anxiously arched, the chin lifted in defiance, and a generous mouth he would have been happy to explore. She would do.

"Catch me, Mommy!" the little girl said, her tiny skirt flaring as she launched herself from the seat toward her mother.

The woman cried out, "Daisy, wait!" But it was too late.

Mike suddenly realized the woman wasn't going to get turned around in time to catch the kid. He took a half step closer and intercepted the little girl, his large, leather-gloved hands folding around her.

"Be careful!" the woman said, reaching for her child.

I'm not a brute. Even if I look like one, he thought bitterly. It took him a moment to understand that the woman wasn't speaking to him but to the little girl.

"Okay, Mommy," the child said as she snuggled her face against his chest.

Mike was surprised by the girl's willingness to trust him. But then, she hadn't seen his face.

"Hold on tight to Mittens," the woman said.

Mike was confused because the little girl's mittens were already on her hands. However, she had a lumpy sweater grasped tightly against her tiny chest. He was startled when the kid leaned her head back, looked him in the eye, and started talking.

"Grampa's truck got broken, and Mommy said *someone* would come. It's really cold. Are you going to help us?"

"Looks like it." Mike felt like smiling but he hadn't in so long, it felt strange even to consider it. Her chatter reminded him of his nephew, when he'd been around this age.

The woman grasped his arm to steady herself as she pulled the hood up on the little girl's coat. The child's mother was a tiny thing, her head barely reaching his shoulders. She met his gaze with worried eyes and said, "Can you take us to the nearest gas station?"

"Nothing will be open in this storm. You better come with me."

He saw concern in her eyes, but also the realization that she didn't have much choice. He was the one with a working vehicle. He was dictating the terms of her rescue. Her hesitation gave him time to look her over more closely.

She was wearing a coat, but it wasn't a warm one, and

her head was uncovered, her long blond hair whipping about her in the wind. Her legs were encased in denim jeans, and she was wearing cowboy boots. *Definitely not dressed for the weather,* he thought.

The little girl's coat was warmer than her mother's, but her tiny legs were merely encased in pink tights and white tennis shoes. The child's blond hair was contained in two pigtails that made it possible to clearly see her large blue eyes and button nose.

The woman flashed him a brief, weary smile and said, "I'm so grateful to you for stopping. We don't want to impose. If you could just take us back to Whitefish—"

He could see she was shivering and interrupted her to say, "Let's get out of this wind." He turned without another word and headed for his pickup with the little girl in his arms. It took a moment before he heard the snow crunching as the woman followed him.

He crossed to the passenger's side of his truck and opened the door, easing the little girl toward the middle of the bench seat. It quickly became clear that her mother was so cold her hands and feet weren't working well. He gripped either side of her slender waist and lifted her into the truck. A woman this good-looking probably had a husband out there somewhere, which made him wonder why the damn fool had sent his wife and child out alone in this dangerous weather.

The woman made a surprised sound as she landed on the bench seat but quickly scooted inside.

"Buckle up," he ordered. "The kid, too."

"My phone died," she said before he closed the door. "If I could use yours, I could call someone—"

"Won't do any good. Nobody's leaving town to come out here in the middle of a blizzard. I wouldn't even have been on the road, except I thought I might get snowed in and decided to get some supplies from town."

He started to shut the passenger's door, but she held out a hand and cried, "Wait!"

"What is it?"

"Our suitcases, mine and my daughter's. They're in the bed of the pickup. Could you get them?"

Mike didn't think anyone was going to steal them in this weather, but if the storm was as bad as the weatherman had predicted, the two of them were going to be staying with him long enough to need a change of clothes.

"I'll be right back," he said, closing her inside the truck. He retrieved a small suitcase and a backpack, which was all he could find, and dumped them in the back seat of his pickup. By the time he got inside, the woman had buckled the little girl in the middle of the bench seat and was working on her own seat belt. He belted himself in, checked to see there was no oncoming traffic, and got back on the road.

In the short time he'd been stopped, night had fallen with a vengeance. With the blowing snow, the headlights weren't doing much to show him the highway. He slowed down to a crawl, afraid he'd miss the turnoff to his cabin.

"I'd be grateful if you could take us to the nearest gas station," she said.

He shook his head. "Nearest station is back the other way. My home is closer."

She shot him an anxious look.

It dawned on him that, despite the desperate weather,

she was afraid of ending up alone with him. He couldn't really blame her. There were *real* monsters out there preying on helpless women. Besides having a nightmare face, he was a very big man, six foot five in his stocking feet, with broad shoulders that looked even bigger in his shearling coat. There wasn't much he could do to alleviate her fear except to explain that the two of them were out of choices.

"Visibility in this storm is bad and getting worse," he said. "We'll be lucky to make it to my place."

Even inching along, he almost missed the turnoff from the highway onto the narrow dirt road that led to his cabin. The drifts were higher along the road cut through the forest, and the truck struggled to make it through a particularly deep bank of drifted snow. He edged to one side, where the passage seemed easier, watching carefully to make sure he didn't scrape one of the myriad aspens and pines and spruces that bordered the road.

"Oh, no!" the little girl cried. "Mittens!"

Mike felt sharp claws digging into his thigh and flashed back to the grizzly attack. His breath caught in his throat as he battled the panic that threatened, struggling to calm himself as he'd been taught. It didn't work. He was suffocating, every bit of life-giving oxygen snagged in his constricted chest. He suddenly smelled the grizzly's fetid breath as its jaws closed over his head.

Something furry launched itself at him, and piercing claws raked the tender flesh at his throat. He heard a startled gasp from the other side of the cab as something heavy caught in his scarf and wrenched it down, revealing his face in all its horror.

Mike went berserk, his PTSD taking over and sending him back to the life or death brawl he'd fought with the grizzly. He yanked at the scarf, which felt like it was strangling him, thrusting it roughly aside, which is when he saw the kitten—*kitten!*—go flying onto the dashboard.

"Goddammit!" he yelled.

Panting, his heart pounding hard enough to burst, he stomped on the brake. Except, his foot hit the accelerator. They plowed into the closest pine tree hard enough to crush the front end of the pickup. The engine clanked once and died, leaving them sitting in the dark.

A small voice beside him said, "Uh-oh."

Chapter 2

Joanna Henderson bit back a scream when she glimpsed the horribly scarred face of the monster sitting at the wheel. Her heart skittered when, an instant later, she felt a rough jolt, heard a crunch of metal, and the pickup was plunged into utter darkness. No airbags deployed in the rusted-out pickup. Joanna could see nothing. *Nothing.* What she heard was little comfort—the stranger breathing harshly across from her, the ping of sleet against the windshield, and an eerie sound she thought must be tree limbs rustling in the vicious wind. She sat paralyzed, suddenly aware that she and her daughter, Daisy, were trapped in the middle of nowhere, in a vehicle that wasn't going anywhere, with a frightening man she didn't know and didn't trust.

Her first thought was escape, but to where? The stranger had turned off the highway five minutes ago. Could she find her way back to the main road through the enfolding forest? How much farther would they have to walk through the pitch-black night, in a life-threatening blizzard, to reach her battered pickup? She and Daisy would likely have frostbite before they found her ice-cold truck, which had sputtered to a stop after she'd ignored the red "check engine" light. Her heart pounded as her pulse raced, and a frisson of fear froze her breath in her chest.

Oh, God. What should I do?

The big man had shown his intentions were good by rescuing them, hadn't he? But were they safe with him? Or in awful peril? Why hadn't he introduced himself? Not knowing his name made his looming figure seem even more ominous.

I should have stopped in Whitefish. But panic had kept her moving. It seemed she'd left the frying pan and jumped right into the fire. Except, that had to be the world's worst metaphor, considering her freezing hands and feet.

The giant sitting across from her was muttering something Joanna couldn't understand. She swallowed over the knot of fear in her throat and asked, "Are you okay?"

A gruff male voice replied, "Are you?" He hesitated, then asked, "Is she?"

Joanna felt around for her daughter in the dark and found her still belted in. "The seat belts saved us."

"I lost Mittens," Daisy wailed. "Where is she?"

Joanna released her seat belt and scooted forward, reaching out with trembling hands toward the dashboard, where she'd last seen the kitten. The feline must have seen her grappling in the dark, because it brushed up against her. She captured the kitten and settled it in Daisy's lap. "Hold her close and don't let go," she said.

"I will," Daisy promised.

"Damned cat," the stranger muttered.

"I didn't think a tiny kitten would be a problem," Joanna said.

He made a disgruntled sound, then asked, "Where's my scarf?"

"On the dash, I think. Do you want me to see if I can–"

"I'll find it myself."

She could understand why he was anxious to cover his face again. Daisy must not have seen his terrible scars in all the commotion and now, blessedly, his gruesome face was hidden from her daughter in the dark. Joanna repressed a shudder of repulsion. And another of pity. Poor man. Surely, with all the modern medical advancements these days, his features could have been made less awful. But maybe he'd had several operations already, and this was the best that could be done.

"What happens now?" she asked.

"We walk to my cabin," he said abruptly.

"How far is it?" Joanna asked.

"A quarter mile."

Joanna wasn't sure if the shiver that shook her body was caused by the thought of trudging so far in the daunting weather or the knowledge that she was going to end up in some isolated cabin with this very brusque, very large man. She reminded herself that, whatever he looked like, he'd likely saved both her life and her daughter's.

"I'm Joanna Henderson," she said. "And this is Daisy," she added, reaching out in the dark to make contact with her daughter's shoulder, comforting them both.

Before he could tell her his name, Daisy said, "I'm cold. Can we go now?"

"Sure, kid," the stranger said.

Joanna could hear movement in the darkness, then felt something heavy land in her lap. "What's this?"

"Blanket," he said. "That coat you have on is useless. Wrap yourself up."

"I'd rather use it for Daisy," she said.

"I've got another blanket for her."

"I'm cold," Daisy reminded them both.

"I know, kid. Give me a minute, and I'll have you snug as a bug in a rug."

Daisy laughed. "Did you hear, Mommy? You say that, too."

Joanna was surprised that the gruff stranger had used an expression usually intended for children. "Do you have a family at your cabin?"

"No."

She waited for some further explanation, but all she heard was the rustle of the blanket as he enveloped Daisy in musty wool. Then he said, "I picked up a small suitcase and a backpack from the bed of your pickup. Can you carry them?"

"I can manage with just the backpack, and I can carry it," she said. Without another word, he dropped the backpack in her lap.

A moment later, he scooped Daisy into his arms, opened the door, and told her, "Hang on to your cat."

A frigid draft and blowing snow shot through the truck cab, and Joanna realized he expected her to follow him. She quickly slid her arms into the straps of the backpack, then wrapped the scratchy blanket around her shoulders, holding it tight against her throat with her gloved hands. She shoved open her door and dropped into two feet of snow. The powdery stuff seeped into her boots and melted, wetting her socks.

She gritted her teeth to keep from yelping. She hadn't thought her feet could get any colder, but as they began their trek, ice crystals formed on her damp socks.

"Stay close," he said.

"I can't see anything."

He flicked on a flashlight bright enough to show her the entire width of the road, highlighting the snow flurries that made it difficult to see more than a few feet in front of them. Apparently, he'd gotten more than blankets from the backseat of the pickup, because he had a bulky bag hanging from a strap over his shoulder.

"Thank goodness you had a flashlight," Joanna said, her teeth chattering. She was glad to see he had Daisy completely covered with a blanket and tucked close to his chest. She had trouble keeping up with the stranger's long strides, but she wasn't about to complain. The sooner they got out of this storm, the better.

Daisy never stopped talking. Joanna knew her daughter was precocious, with an unusually large vocabulary. But she heard her daughter saying things she'd had no idea the four-and-a-half-year-old had overheard, let alone understood, much less remembered. Her cold ears burned as she listened.

"We used to live in Texas. Mommy's been driving and driving and driving about a hundred miles. I got a kitty 'cause my dog, Roxie, died. She ate poison and got sick all over the floor and Mommy had to clean it up. Mommy says I'm smart as a whip, but I'm a big 'sponsabilty. Do you like cats?"

Joanna fought both tears and laughter as he replied, "No."

If he thought being terse was going to shut Daisy up, he was sadly mistaken.

"I got a kitty 'cause cats aren't as much work as dogs. Mommy makes the best cookies in the world. Do you want her to make some for you?"

"No."

"They taste really good. Are we almost there?"

"Yes," he said, adding under his breath, "Thank God."

Joanna nearly sobbed with relief when his light flashed across the front of a small cabin made of logs. By the time they could see the house, they were only a few steps from the covered porch. She was surprised when the stranger simply shoved open the door and stepped inside, but this godforsaken place was so far from any beaten path he probably didn't need to lock it up when he was gone. No one who didn't know this cabin existed would be likely to stumble across it.

Which reminded her how perilous her situation was. If things went sideways, no one was going to show up out of the blue to rescue her from her rescuer. She wondered if the stranger had a charger that would work on her phone, or a land line, and whether he would let her use them if he did.

But who would she call? She'd cut all ties in Texas, running as fast and as far as she could from the threat that awaited her there.

It was warmer inside than it was outside, but not by much. Apparently, the stranger had turned the heat way down when he left. She saw him flip a switch by the door, which she assumed was for the lights, but nothing happened. He flipped it again and muttered, "Shit!"

"Uh-oh. Mommy says that's a bad word."

He turned and forced Daisy into Joanna's arms. "Hold her while I see if it's just a fuse or whether the power is out."

Joanna had to drop her blanket to catch Daisy, who wrapped her legs around her mother's waist to keep from sliding to the floor. The stranger disappeared into another room, taking the flashlight with him, leaving her standing in the dark.

A moment later he was back, but without the sack of whatever he'd carried on a strap across his shoulder. "Power's out. Let me get a fire started. The fireplace isn't big enough to heat the whole house, so we'll have to bunk down in here tonight."

Joanna wasn't sure whether to feel relieved or not.

He headed for the stack of wood beside the fireplace. When he bent down, his scarf slid away, and the flashlight in his hand angled enough to reveal his features.

"Uh-oh," Daisy said, pointing at his face. "You have a boo-boo."

Chapter 3

Mike dropped the flashlight, which noisily rolled away on the hardwood floor, and instinctively reached up to pull the scarf more securely around his face. He'd already covered himself before he realized the child hadn't screamed. Hadn't cried. Hadn't even sounded particularly surprised. She'd called his horrible scars a "boo boo."

He turned to the woman, only his blazing eyes visible, seeing in her face the horror he'd expected to find in the child's, and demanded, "Why isn't she scared of me?"

"I don't know."

Mike turned away from the two of them, completely unsettled, and sought solace in the familiar task of building the fire. He'd lost electricity in the past, so he always made sure kindling was laid in the fireplace before he left the house. All he needed to start the fire was an extra log and a match.

"Make yourselves comfortable," he said without turning around, gesturing toward a couple of chintz wing chairs chosen by his sister-in-law when she'd lived here five years ago. The chairs were set perpendicular to the fire, across from a flower-patterned couch. "There's a hob at the fireplace where I can hang a pot, so once the fire gets going, I can make hot chocolate."

"I *love* hot chocolate," the little girl said. "With tiny marshmallows."

"No marshmallows."

The kid scrunched up her face and said, "Awwww."

"That sounds wonderful," the woman said with a grateful smile. "Even without the marshmallows."

The girl's mother sounded friendly enough, but he noticed she hadn't moved an inch farther inside the room. Her daughter might not be scared of him, but Mike was pretty sure his unwelcome visitor didn't feel the least bit safe.

His fearsome looks weren't helped by his shaggy black hair or the thick beard he'd grown in a futile attempt to hide the scars around his mouth and chin. There was no way to conceal the puckered white lines on his forehead that ran through his right eyebrow and down across the edge of his mouth. Or the jagged marks on his hands, for that matter.

Now that he knew the kid wasn't going to make a fuss, he might as well get rid of his hat and gloves and scarf. They would need their coats until the fire heated up the room. He reached up to unwind the scarf from around his throat and paused. The kid might not mind what she saw, but he knew the lady would. The thick wool scarf hid the damage—hell, the total devastation—caused by the grizzly to what had once been an okay face. According to a few women he'd known, a more than okay face, he thought with regret.

It was too bad he hadn't found himself a wife before

his looks had been ruined. But at the time of the attack he'd only been twenty-three, not nearly ready to settle down. It had occurred to him over the past five years he'd spent alone—his brother said *hiding out*—that even a woman who loved him might have trouble looking at him across the breakfast table for the rest of her life.

The scarf stayed where it was. Mike stuck his gloves in the pocket of his shearling coat, then crossed to the antler rack inside the door to hang up his Stetson.

The woman took a step sideways to keep an equal distance between them. He moved back toward the fireplace to give her the room she seemed to need to keep from feeling threatened.

"It's a lot warmer over by the fire," he said.

He saw the woman's reluctance to get anywhere near him, but when the little girl visibly shivered, the woman headed for the chair closest to the fire. She set down her daughter, let the blanket drop to the floor, then slipped off her backpack and dropped it on the floor beside her, before settling into the chair and dragging the little girl and her kitten into her lap.

"I'm tired, Mommy," the girl said, her head drooping against her mother's shoulder.

"I know, sweetheart." The woman met his gaze, which he could see took an effort, and said, "Would you mind if I lay her down on the couch and cover her up with the blankets?"

"Go ahead."

He watched the exhausted woman remove the little girl's—her name was *Daisy,* he reminded himself—sparkly tennis shoes before she rose, crossed to the couch, and settled her daughter there with one of the decorative couch pillows under her head. After she'd removed the kitten from Daisy's arms, setting it free to investigate the room, she wrapped the tiny girl up in the blanket and murmured, "Snug as a bug in a rug."

He heard the child's bell-like laugh before she said, "G'night, Mommy." And then, to his surprise, "G'night, Mister Man."

Mike wasn't sure why he'd been so stingy about sharing his name, but he didn't want to spend the next 48 to 72 hours, depending on the duration of the storm, stuck in this cabin being called "Mister Man." He met the little girl's heavy-eyed gaze and said, "I'm Mike." He glanced at the woman, who was staring at him with surprise, and said, "Mike Sullivan."

"G'night, Mike," the child said. "Should I say my prayers now, Mommy?"

The woman, *Joanna,* he corrected himself, shot a look at him over her shoulder, checking where he was in the room, before she turned back and said, "Sure, sweetheart."

The two of them repeated a simple children's prayer that ended with Daisy blessing a long list of people including her cat. Toward the end he heard, "And my new friend Mike. Amen."

Joanna kissed her daughter's forehead, both cheeks, and then her puckered, rosebud mouth before she rose and faced him, obviously unsure what to do next. She crossed her arms protectively over her chest and said, "My hands and feet are frozen solid."

"You don't want to thaw them too quickly, or you might do some damage. Best to stand a little way off from the fire."

He could see her reluctance to come anywhere near him, but her teeth chattered, and she apparently decided she needed the heat more than she feared the man in the room with her.

They stood close to each other without speaking long enough that the silence became uncomfortable. Finally, she blurted, "What happened to your face?"

He hadn't expected her to be so blunt. Most people just gaped, then walked away as quickly as they could. He gave her an answer that often raised as many questions as it answered. "Grizzly attack."

He watched her eyes widen in shock. Being attacked by a grizzly was even more rare than being attacked by a shark, a unique experience suffered by very few humans. Being clawed by a five-hundred pound bear in the wild just didn't happen all that often to normal folks.

Joanna was still gawking, so he added, "My brother and I have a ranch, the Rafter S, near here. I was looking for some missing cattle in the forest and surprised a grizzly eating one of our Black Angus calves." He shrugged. "Bad-tempered fellow objected to my interrupting his lunch."

Mike had spoken in a calm voice, but whenever he recounted the attack, gooseflesh rose on his arms, and his stomach clenched in remembered fear. He was a former SEAL and had seen comrades die in battle. He'd been wounded in combat himself and had ended up with a metal plate in his shoulder that resulted in his medical discharge from the Navy. He'd never once suffered PTSD as a result of his combat experience in Afghanistan. But the grizzly attack replayed in his dreams so often, he rarely got a decent night's sleep.

He expected her to ask all the usual questions, like how had he escaped with his life? What had happened to the grizzly? Instead, she completely changed the subject. "The décor here isn't what I expected," she said, glancing at the chintz fabrics on the furniture. "This place belongs to my sister-in-law. When Vick married my brother, Rye, five years ago, she offered it to me. I just never got around to moving her stuff out." Vick had somehow understood he needed privacy to adjust to his new circumstances.

Like having the face of a monster.

Mike had been told again and again that he shouldn't think that way. His mother and her second husband, his older brother and sister-in-law, and younger sister and brother-in-law, all pretended there was nothing wrong with his looks. Not even his nephews and nieces shrank from him in horror, unless he caught them off-guard.

He'd never replaced Vick's furnishings with his own because he'd never imagined he'd be living here by himself for so long. But five years later, he was still a lone wolf licking his wounds. He spent his nights reading, imagining a life far different from the one he was actually living. He yearned to travel. He yearned to have a family of his own. He yearned . . . . for a lot of things he feared he would never have.

Sometimes, he could forget for as much as a day that his features had been forever altered. Then something would happen, like needing to rescue a woman and her child from the side of the road, and he would be reminded that the face he presented to the world created fear in people's hearts.

He saw Joanna shiver and realized she must be a lot

colder than he'd suspected or she'd admitted. He took a step toward her, and she shrank back.

"Stand still." He modulated his voice to make it less intimidating and said, "I'm not going to hurt you, Joanna. I just want to help."

He could tell it was taking all the courage she had not to run as he closed the short distance between them. He took one of her arms by the wrist and eased it away from her body far enough to remove her sorry excuse for a glove. Her fingers were in even worse shape than he'd thought.

"Sit down on the rug," he said.

The "rug" was an expensive Persian carpet. Until he could scrape up the cash to buy this place from his sister-in-law, he didn't feel like he had the right to get rid of the feminine furnishings. Besides, he kept telling himself, he was going to move on someday soon, so what was the point?

Except, he kept putting that day off. Fear, dread, simple inertia had kept him locked in step right where he was. Seeing his ruined face reflected in this attractive woman's wide-set blue eyes was a reminder of why he avoided people whenever he could.

Joanna sank cross-legged onto the carpet, and he joined her there. He held out his hand and said, "Take off that other glove, and give me your hands."

She hesitated only a moment before awkwardly following his instructions. He put her hands together, palm to palm, then covered her icy hands with his warm ones. He didn't rub, knowing how painful that would be, just sat there, flesh-to-flesh, waiting for her fingers to feel human again.

It was the first time in a long time he'd touched a female who wasn't a relative. Four years and nine months to be precise—from the grizzly attack in mid-March four years ago to this mid-December night. Christmas was two weeks away, not that you could tell from his cabin, which didn't have a single decoration to mark the occasion. He'd been having a hard time feeling the joy of the season.

Joanna was looking everywhere except at him. Down at their joined hands, over to the flickering fire, up to the mantel covered with female bric-a-brac, to the French impressionistic art over the fireplace, then back to her hands encased in his.

"Your hands are really warm," she murmured.

He smiled with amusement, then remembered what his smile looked like in the mirror and relaxed his features. "I'm just the right temperature. Your hands are freezing cold."

She shot him a half smile. "Not nearly as cold as my feet."

He let go of her hands, shifted backwards on his butt, and reached for one of her booted feet.

"What are you doing?"

"I need to take off your boots and socks and get a look at your feet."

"Oh," she said in a small voice. She straightened out her legs so he could pull off her boots.

"Your socks are frozen stiff!" He eased them off, and when he saw her frostbitten feet said in disgust, "Why didn't you say something sooner?" He left her sitting there while he jumped up, causing her to gasp in alarm and him to flinch, before he headed into the kitchen.

Her feet needed more than warm hands. They needed

warm, not hot, water to thaw them out. He returned with a kettle filled with water, which he put on the hob and eased over the fire. "There's no hot water from the faucet, so we'll need to heat some. Meanwhile, I'll do what I can to warm up your feet."

He unbuttoned his coat and shrugged it off, then began unbuttoning his long-sleeved black-and-red plaid wool shirt.

He'd freed no more than two buttons before she looked up at him with startled blue eyes and said, "What are you doing now?"

It was easier to show her than to tell her. He settled on the floor across from her, his long legs spread on either side of her, shoved up his long johns shirt, grasped her ankles, and set both of her feet flat against his belly.

He hissed and said, "Damn, lady, you weren't kidding. Your feet are frozen!"

She sucked in a breath and then let it out with a sigh. It had obviously not occurred to her that he might use his hair-swirled belly to warm her feet.

"Are you always like this?" she asked in a quiet voice.

"If I'd told you what I planned to do, you might have refused. In the long run, that could've cost you a toe or two. I figured it was better to act first and explain later."

"Thank you, Mike. But next time, ask."

Mike realized that having a woman this close, even though it was only her cold feet pressed against his muscled abdomen, was causing an unwanted response in another part of his body. It surprised him, because he'd thought maybe the grizzly attack had killed that part of his psyche, too. This was the first time he'd been aroused by a woman for longer than he wanted to remember. And it was coming at a pretty damned inconvenient time.

He shifted away, removing her feet, so she wouldn't see the growing ridge in his jeans. "I think that water ought to be warm enough now. I'll get a pail so you can soak your feet. Go sit in one of the chairs. I'll be right back."

Mike Sullivan, the big bad man who frightened children simply by looking in their direction, turned and ran, putting as much distance as he could between himself and temptation.

Chapter 4

Joanna heard Mittens yowl and Mike swear. "Is everything all right?" she called from the living room, keeping her voice low so she wouldn't wake Daisy.

"Everything's fine," he called back from the kitchen. "I tripped over the cat. It ran off, so it's probably okay. I'll set up something it can use as a sandbox."

Joanna couldn't believe they were having such an ordinary conversation. She struggled to curb the survival instinct that urged her to grab her child and run as far and as fast as she could. Mike Sullivan had been nothing but helpful so far. But he was too big. Too intimidating. Too fearsome.

Joanna was five foot four in her stocking feet and weighed in at 112 pounds. In any physical contest between them, she was going to lose. She'd been too grateful to be in out of the cold to focus on that fact. It had been brought home to her with startling clarity when she noticed—how could she miss it with her feet settled on his belly—the thick ridge that appeared between his legs, ominously stretching the fabric of his jeans.

If Mike Sullivan decided he wanted her, there was nothing she could do to stop him.

She'd exhaled a *whoosh* of relief when he'd left the room. The problem was he'd be coming back.

Joanna looked around for anything she could use as a weapon. There were fire irons by the fireplace, but she couldn't conceal something like that until it was needed. She rose with difficulty and took a few careful, excruciatingly painful steps toward the mantel on her frozen feet, looking for some piece of bric-a-brac she could smash against his head.

"What are you doing?"

She jerked at the sound of his voice, and the china figurine she'd been reaching for went flying, splintering into a thousand pieces when it landed on the river rock at the base of the fireplace. She whimpered as she whirled, her hands up, palms out, to protect herself.

Nothing happened. The only sound in the darkened room was her own frantic breathing.

Then she heard Mike's baritone voice, low and calm, saying, "Go back to sleep, Daisy. Everything's fine."

She lowered her hands in time to see him set down a metal pan on an end table, pull off some oven mitts, then gently rearrange the blanket around Daisy's shoulders.

His features were blank, his eyes hooded, revealing nothing of what he was feeling. She figured he must have perfected that neutral guise over the years of dealing with apprehensive looks from strangers.

"Your feet must be hurting," he said. "Are you ready to soak them now?"

Wasn't he going to say something about the broken figurine? Or her gasp of panic? Or her defensive posture?

Apparently not.

He headed straight for her, and she felt her heart skitter in an effort to escape her chest. She folded her fisted hands close to her body and held herself rigid, determined to fight him. But all he did was scoop her up in his arms, carry her across the room, and dump her in one of the chintz wing chairs.

"You were about to step on some glass," he said.

She shot him a frustrated look. "You could have said that before you picked me up."

He merely shrugged before collecting the pan, which he dropped on the carpet in front of her. He crossed the room to recover the mitts and dragged them back on, then picked up the heavy black pot from the hob. He filled the wide, shallow pan at her feet with warm water, before putting the pot back where he'd found it.

She watched with wary eyes as he took off the mitts, crossed back to her, and brushed his fingertips through the water.

"Just right," he said.

When he reached for one of her ankles she said, "I can do it."

He stood there holding the ridiculous mitts, waiting for her to lift her feet and set them in the pan.

She bit back an agonized groan as she settled first one foot, and then the other, into the warm water. Her thawing feet felt like they were being pricked with a million needles.

It hurt. A lot.

As she sat there suffering, she was aware of how close

he was standing. He towered over her. She felt foolish for feeling threatened, when he hadn't threatened her, but asked, "Would you mind stepping back?"

She saw the flicker of something in his eyes and a twitch that curled his lip in what might have been disgust or disdain, before he took two steps backward.

"I'll get rid of that broken glass and make us some hot chocolate." He reclaimed the pot from the hob and carried it into the kitchen. He was back a few moments later with a broom and dustpan and swept up the mess she'd made. "Hot chocolate coming up," he said as he headed back to the kitchen.

Joanna was suddenly ravenous. She couldn't remember the last time she and Daisy had eaten. Too long ago. She'd kept driving, hoping to outrun the storm. And she'd been conserving funds. She only had enough money left to get the truck fixed and maybe spend a night or two in a motel in town. Her mouth was salivating at the thought of drinking something hot and sweet.

Then she realized Mike was making his concoction in the kitchen, where she couldn't see what he put into it. What if he drugged her?

You're being silly, Joanna. That man has done nothing to deserve that sort of suspicion. If Mike Sullivan was going to take advantage of you, he would already have done it. If you think about it, he seemed almost embarrassed that his body responded that way. He got up and left the room, for heaven's sake! Is that the behavior of a man who plans to ravish you?

He was back with the kettle and settled it on the hob, his hands once again encased in the absurdly feminine oven mitts. Once the kettle was on the fire, he pulled the mitts off and turned to face her.

She couldn't help the anxious sound that escaped her throat when he took a step in her direction.

He stopped in his tracks and muttered, "He must be one hell of a bastard."

"What did you say?"

"The man you're running from. The one who hit you."

Her mouth fell open, and her hand unconsciously rose to her cheek. "What?"

"Whatever makeup you were using to cover that bruise is gone," he said flatly. "You had your hands up to keep me from hitting you when I was still six feet away. I'm not him. I've never hit a woman, or hurt a woman, in my life. I don't appreciate your treating me like I'm Godzilla on the rampage."

His voice had never gotten loud, but she was left in no doubt about how angry he was. An angry man was terrifying. Except, he was furious because she *wouldn't, couldn't, didn't* believe he had no intention of hurting her.

And for good reason. Men lied.

Every man she'd ever cared about had lied right to her face. Her father, who'd promised when she was eleven years old that he would "be home soon" from a business trip to Houston but never returned to his wife and daughter. Tommie Ray Johnson, the teenage boy who'd promised he'd love her forever, and walked away when he got her pregnant her freshman year at college. And John Thomas Tennant, the man she'd believed was her one true love, who knew how she felt about liars, and lied to her anyway, just like her father and her Baylor University boyfriend.

J.T. had sworn he would never hit her again. And then had broken that promise. Promised again and broken his word again. She'd loved him, or thought she did. So she'd forgiven him and stayed with him. It had taken his raising a hand to strike Daisy to bring her to her senses. Joanna had leapt between the supposed love of her life and her daughter, taking the blow on her back that had been meant for Daisy's face. In that instant, Joanna had made up her mind that she was done with him.

Except, nothing was ever easy with J.T. Not even leaving him.

Joanna had a bank account in her name, but J.T. had convinced her to quit her job as a paralegal, so it didn't have much cash in it. He'd talked her into using credit cards in his name, so she'd let hers lapse. He'd bought her a new car, so she'd sold her old one. She'd given up her apartment and lived with J.T. in a high-rise condominium in Austin that had security at the front door, reporting every time she went in or out. He paid for her phone and insisted on having the password "just in case."

It had all been done so subtly, it wasn't until she wanted to walk away that Joanna realized she had no assets, no credit cards, no automobile, no home, no phone, nothing at all in her own name. It was all paid for by J.T.

He'd been livid when she'd told him she was leaving him. Apparently, no woman had ever walked out on J.T. If anyone was going to do the leaving, he'd shouted, it would be him. And he wasn't done with Joanna. He warned her that he'd find her if she tried to run, that she belonged to him.

Joanna had wondered aloud why any man would want

a woman in his bed who despised him. That was when he'd struck her cheek hard enough to leave a bruise. It was the third time he'd hit her, and Joanna had determined it would be the last.

Leaving J.T. had required planning. Especially since he made her account for everything she did, everywhere she went. He refused to let her take Daisy on errands, knowing she would never leave without her daughter. Without her grandfather's help, escape would have been impossible. Gramps had given her his '57 Dodge, offered her what little cash he had on hand to buy gas, filled a cooler with food and drinks, hugged her and Daisy one last time, and sent them on their way.

Joanna realized she was half asleep, slumped in the chintz chair, but it would have taken too much effort to sit upright again. Despite the possible danger, exhaustion had taken its toll. Her eyes slid closed.

She didn't resist when she felt her feet gently lifted from the warm water and dried with a soft towel, before being settled back on the carpet.

She remembered putting her arm around a powerful shoulder as she was lifted out of the chair and settled flat on the carpet in front of the fireplace, her head on a soft pillow. She felt a blanket being tucked around her as she turned her face toward the warmth of the fire.

Then she heard the quiet, comforting words, "Snug as a bug in a rug."

Chapter 5

Mike felt something poke his arm and jerked awake, ready to defend himself. He struggled to draw breath, his eyes searching the near-darkness for danger. For a moment, he didn't know where he was. Then he remembered he'd settled into one of the chintz wing chairs, since Daisy was sleeping on the couch and Joanna was stretched out in front of the fire. Steel-gray light streamed through the top half of the living room window. The bottom half was covered in drifted snow. He put a fisted hand to his chest to quiet his racing heart.

"Damned PTSD," he muttered. Then he spied Daisy standing quietly next to his chair. She was holding the kitten clutched to her chest.

"Are you awake, Mike?" she whispered.

"I am now," he said with a rueful smile, as he set his trembling hands on his thighs. "Why are we whispering?"

"Mommy's still asleep," she said, setting the kitten on the arm of the chair and pointing toward her mother, who was wrapped up in a blanket in front of the fireplace. "I'm hungry," she said. "And I need to go to the potty."

Because Mike's brother had possessed sole custody of his son from the day Cody was born, Mike had helped care for his nephew the first five years of his life. He'd diapered him, clothed him, bathed him, fed him, babysat him, played with him, done everything a good uncle, who lived in the same household, would do. So he had plenty of experience with raising a little boy. But this was a little *girl*.

The kitten had nestled in his lap. He didn't want the cat making a habit of it, so he gently set it on the carpet at his feet. It immediately began purring and brushing against his Levi's. His family had always had dogs. He had no experience with cats and didn't understand why this one seemed to like him, when he didn't particularly like it. He would have to be careful not to squash the damn thing with his stocking feet when he stood up.

Daisy laid a firmer hand on his sleeve—it must have been her touch that had woken him—and looked up at him with blue eyes so round and innocent he felt his heart melt. He reminded himself the little girl was only passing through his life. No sense asking for trouble by letting himself get any more involved than he already was with her or her mother.

His inclination was to wake Joanna to take care of the kid's needs. But if Joanna was still sleeping, it was probably because she needed the rest. He ought to be able to get Daisy in and out the bathroom and feed her breakfast without her mother's help.

The instant he rose, being careful to step over the cat, Daisy stretched out a hand, and Mike engulfed her tiny fingers in his. He couldn't help marveling at her complete disregard of his looks. She acted like his scarred face didn't have the appearance of a gargoyle, as though it were normal, when he knew it wasn't. He didn't understand her willingness to ignore what so many others, adults and children, found revolting. It felt strange to be treated like a regular human being.

But he liked it. He liked it a lot.

Mike led Daisy down the hall to the bathroom and stepped inside with her. Fortunately, there was enough light from the window to see the toilet. The seat was up, and he set it down as quietly as he could. "The seat'll be cold," he warned.

Without waiting for him to leave, she began pulling down her pink tights. She got them down, along with her panties, then surveyed the toilet, held up her arms, and said, "Can you help me, please?"

He immediately understood her problem. Cody had a stool he'd used to stand on to pee, in the years before he was tall enough to reach the bowl. A little girl had to climb up to sit on the seat. There was no stool, and she was too small to reach the toilet on her own.

He caught her under the arms and settled her on the seat, waiting to make sure she had a good hold on it before he let go.

"*Brrr,*" she said with a laugh. "It's cold!"

He realized that the way she was holding on with two hands so she wouldn't fall in, she was going to have a problem reaching the toilet paper, so he rolled a little off and held it out to her.

When she was done, she matter-of-factly took it, wiped herself, then reached up to him so he could help her back onto her feet. He caught her hand before she could flush, lowered the lid and said, "We'll do that later," since he didn't want the noise to wake Joanna.

Mike watched Daisy struggle for a moment to pull up her underwear and tights before he knelt to help her sort them out. Underwear first. Then tights. When both were where they belonged, he used a wet wipe to clean her hands, which was a lot quieter, considering the way his bathroom pipes complained in the winter, than turning on the water. When he was done, she slid her arms around his neck, and he rose with her clasped to his chest, her legs wrapped around him.

He'd forgotten how loving a child could be when not shrinking from him in horror. This sort of trust was what had been missing from his life over the past five years.

"I guess you need breakfast," he said. Except, he had no electricity to cook anything. "How about a bowl of cereal?" he suggested. And then realized that he hadn't bought milk, only cream, and the only cereal he had was oatmeal, which needed to be cooked. "Or we can make toast over the fire."

"Can I have mine with peanut butter and banana?"

"I don't have any bananas." *Or peanut butter, for that matter.* He pretty much stuck with coffee for breakfast and took a bag lunch to eat wherever he was working on the ranch when noon came around. He skipped dinner or microwaved something from the freezer. "How about some honey on your toast?"

"I *love* honey," she said, smiling up at him. "Can I have coffee with my toast?"

"Your mom lets you drink coffee?" he asked skeptically.

"Just for special times. With lots of cream and sugar. I

think this is a special time, don't you?"

Since the cream had stayed cold in the fridge over-night, and he had sugar, he said, "Coffee it is. We'll have to be quiet so we don't wake your mom."

Daisy was quiet, but she wasn't silent.

"I bet Mittens is hungry," she whispered as he carried her down the hall to the kitchen. "Mommy forgot to bring cat food. But I don't think Mittens will like toast."

Mike glanced at Joanna, who looked dead to the world as they passed through the living room to the kitchen, then asked in a quiet voice, "How about a bowl of cream for Mittens?"

"Mommy gave her cream, and she licked it all up."

"Then cream it is."

He poured the cat a bowl of cream, then tiptoed back to the living room to build up the fire before filling a pot with water and putting it on the hob to boil.

He froze when Joanna turned over, lifted her head without opening her eyes, and asked, "What's going on?"

"Everything's fine," he said.

Her head dropped back onto the pillow as she mur-mured something unintelligible, and a moment later, she was asleep again.

When Mike returned to the kitchen, Daisy stood beside him at the silverware drawer, watching intently as he searched as soundlessly as he could for a fork he could stick into a piece of bread and hold over the fire.

"What are you looking for?" she whispered.

He held up a fork that was part of a knife and fork set for carving a roast and said, "This."

Her eyes went wide. "That's a really big fork."

"Yep." He grabbed the loaf of bread from the top of the fridge, pulled out a slice, and stabbed it onto the fork. He held it up like a trophy and said, "Now we're ready to toast it over the fire."

She grinned up at him. "Can I hold it?"

"I think I better do that, but if you're really quiet, so you don't wake up your mom, you can watch."

"Okay," she whispered.

Mike grabbed a paper towel and a couple more slices of bread and headed back into the living room, trailed by the little girl. Joanna was dead to the world. He figured she must have been traveling a lot longer than a single day to be this far out of it. What kind of man scared a woman into running like a hunted animal?

Daisy shared a look of pure delight with him as they watched the toast turn brown. He set the first piece on the paper towel, which Daisy held in her lap. He toasted three more before he leaned over and said, "Take those to the kitchen. I'll be right behind you with the water for the coffee."

"Okay, Mike," she whispered back.

Mike shot a final look at Joanna before he slipped on the oven mitts and took the pot of boiling water off the hob. The mauve shadows under Joanna's eyes were evidence of why she was able to sleep through sounds that he knew would ordinarily have woken her. He was glad Joanna felt safe enough to finally rest. That meant something to him. Maybe she'd realized there was no reason to be frightened of him.

She may not be scared that you'll harm her, he thought as he carried the pot of water to the kitchen. *But she still hasn't looked you directly in the face. She still doesn't see past the scars to the man behind them. She still doesn't see* you.

Daisy had dropped the paper towel with the four slices of bread onto the kitchen table and opened the silverware drawer. Mike heard the metal clatter when she accidentally dropped a utensil back into the drawer. He glanced over his shoulder to the living room, expecting any second to hear Joanna's voice.

But she slept on.

"I found a knife for the butter," Daisy told him, holding up a table knife the way he'd held up the fork.

"I see that."

He settled the pot on the cold stove, then got mugs from a holder on the counter and used instant coffee to make a cup for each of them. When he turned around, Daisy was gone. He felt a stab of panic and called out, "Daisy? Where are you?"

She didn't answer, just reappeared in the kitchen doorway with something clutched to her chest. "I had to get Bitsy from Mommy's backpack. She'll be hungry, too."

It took Mike a second to realize that she was holding a doll. She brushed the doll's curly blond hair away from its face, tenderly kissed it, then turned it so he could see it. "Bitsy has a boo-boo, too."

Mike hitched in a startled breath, and a chill raced down his spine. The porcelain doll's face had been shattered, as though someone had thrown it against a wall. Or stomped on it. Broken pieces and crushed spots left the doll's face horribly distorted. Like his own.

Mike's hands were shaking. Gooseflesh covered his

arms. No wonder Joanna's daughter could look at him and not be afraid. She'd just kissed a face very much like his own.

"What happened to your doll?" he said past the painfully swollen knot in his throat.

Daisy smoothed a loving hand over the doll's broken face, looked up at him with tears welling in her eyes and said, "She had an accident."

Mike didn't ask for details. But if he ever met the man who'd done this, he'd make sure the son of a bitch knew what it felt like to lose something precious to him.

Daisy dropped onto the blanket Mike had grabbed from the couch and tossed onto the floor near the cat's bowl when he'd brought the pot of hot water back to the kitchen. She laid her doll on it, then began petting the kitten, which was lapping at the bowl of cream.

"I hope Santa Claus can find me here," Daisy said. "I asked for a new doll so Bitsy would have a friend. Bitsy had to leave home, so she doesn't have friends anymore."

Mike realized that Daisy was the one who'd had to leave home. The one who no longer had friends. "Don't worry," he reassured her. "Santa can find you wherever you are."

"Really?" She glanced back toward the living room. "'Cause there's no Christmas tree or stockings by the chimney. How will he know to come here?"

"It's his job to find good little girls."

She shot him a worried look. "Santa might not think I've been good. J.T. said I was a devil from hell."

"What!" Mike was so shocked at the thought of anyone comparing this angelic child to the devil that he'd raised his voice. He waited with bated breath to hear Joanna waking, but there was no sound from the living room. Mike was getting a pretty ugly picture of this J.T. character. He laid a comforting hand on Daisy's shoulder and said, "I'm sure you didn't do anything that will keep Santa away."

"I threw away J.T.'s cigarettes," she said in a small voice. "Mommy said cigarettes can kill you, and I didn't want J.T. to die."

The sad look on Daisy's face would have broken a heart far harder than his own. He picked her up and held her close, wishing he could protect her from all the evil in the world, and said, "Tell you what. We'll put up a tree and hang a stocking, too, so Santa will be sure to find you here."

"What if I'm not here at Christmas?"

"Don't you worry about that. We'll figure something out."

She laid her head on his shoulder and tightened her hands around his neck and gave a relieved sigh that made it clear how worried she'd been. "Okay, Mike."

Those two words revealed her utter confidence, her trust that, if he told her something would be so, it would be so.

Chapter 6

Joanna awoke with a start, realized she couldn't move, and struggled frantically to get free, only to discover it wasn't ropes binding her but a warm blanket. She sank back on the carpet and heaved a sigh of relief. She vaguely remembered waking up and hearing a male voice reassuring her it was okay to sleep some more. She rolled over in her cocoon so she could see the couch, where she expected to find her daughter. Her heart skipped a beat when she realized the couch was empty.

"Daisy!" she cried, shoving wildly at the wool blanket. "Daisy, where are you?"

"I'm in the kitchen, Mommy," her daughter called back. "Me and Mike are eating breakfast."

Daisy stumbled to her feet and bit back a howl of pain. Her feet hurt. To her surprise, they were encased in a pair of wool socks that were so large she suspected they belonged to Mike. He must have slipped them onto her feet after she'd gone to sleep. She was grateful for the extra warmth they provided as she stepped off the Persian carpet and headed across the frigid wood floor to the kitchen.

She was both surprised and relieved to find Daisy sitting happily in Mike's lap, a large coffee cup held carefully in both her tiny hands.

"I ate toast with honey," Daisy announced. "And I'm drinking coffee with cream and sugar."

"You gave a five-year-old coffee?" Joanna said, frowning at Mike.

He shrugged. "I didn't have any milk. Or much of anything else in the fridge to be honest. I wasn't planning on company when I shopped yesterday. She said you let her drink coffee on special occasions."

"I do. But—" Joanna cut herself off. She should be grateful for Mike Sullivan's help, not critical of the way he'd offered it. "Thank you for taking care of Daisy," she said, then couldn't resist adding, "but you should have woken me up." She didn't want to owe this stranger any more than she already did.

"You seemed to need the sleep," he replied. "And we're not going anywhere today." He pointed toward the large window over the farmhouse sink, where sleet rattled against the glass pane. The sun was clearly up but not making much of an appearance. The evergreens surrounding the cabin were heavily laden with snow, which was coming down in large, swirling flakes.

"Do you want some of my toast, Mommy?" Daisy asked, holding out a half-eaten piece of scorched bread.

"No thanks, sweetheart. You finish it up." She focused her gaze on Mike and asked, "Do you have a phone I could use? Or a charger for my cell?"

"The land line is out. What kind of phone do you have?"

"An iPhone."

He shook his head. "I use an android."

"Could I borrow your cell?"

"Who were you planning to call?"

"Uber or Lyft or a cab," she said. "Someone who can pick us up and take us into town."

"Don't waste your time," he replied. "My truck is blocking the road. Harry runs the best garage in Whitefish, and he won't be able to tow it out of the way until this storm is over."

Joanna crossed to stare out the window. The world outside looked cold and bleak. There was no sign of any living thing, animal or human. *If you could get a ride, where were you planning to go, Joanna? You only have enough money for a few days in a motel. You need a job, preferably one that doesn't require a Social Security number. And with this storm keeping everyone at home, who's likely to be hiring?*

She felt helpless and hopeless. She turned to Mike and said, "I guess we'll be imposing on you a little longer."

Joanna suddenly realized she hadn't recoiled from Mike's face when she'd spoken to him, even though he'd done nothing to hide his ragged flesh. Maybe it was the sight of her daughter held protectively in his arms. J.T. would have put Daisy in a chair of her own. It would never have occurred to him to cuddle her child as Mike was doing.

"There's some coffee in a pan on the stove," he said. "Help yourself. I managed to burn some toast over the fire, if you want to give it a try."

Joanna conceded that, if he'd done all that without waking her up, she must have been down for the count. "Thanks. I'm starved. First, where's the bathroom?"

"Down the hall, Mommy. Watch out, 'cause the seat is cold! *Brrrrr.*"

Joanna felt a shiver of anxiety at the thought of her daughter alone with this stranger while she'd been sleeping. "You took her to the bathroom?"

Mike shrugged again. "It was no big deal. She just needed help getting onto the seat."

"Mike used a wet wipe to wash my hands, Mommy." She carefully set down the coffee cup and held up both hands palm out to show they were clean. "Except, now they have honey on them," she said, licking a sticky forefinger.

Mike Sullivan was a little too good to be true, Joanna thought. He seemed like a nice man, but it wouldn't be smart to let down her guard. Not quite yet.

"Excuse me," she said, turning to seek out the bathroom. "I'll be back for that coffee and toast."

By the time Joanna returned, Daisy was playing with Mittens on the carpet near the fireplace. Joanna joined Mike, who was stacking dishes in the dishwasher.

He turned to her and said, "I left toast and butter and jelly for you on the table, and a cup for your coffee, along with sugar and cream."

Joanna realized as she listened to Mike, that instead of the multitude of scars on his face, she was seeing his eyes for the first time. They were blue, with little spikes of black radiating from the pupil. A woman could easily succumb to the lure of those deep blue pools, if she were so inclined. Which

Joanna was *not*.

She poured herself coffee from the pan on the stove, which had apparently been heated on the fire, added cream, then settled at the table, where she lathered butter on a piece of toast and added a purple jelly. She took one bite, closed her eyes, and murmured, "Mmmmm. I had no idea cold toast and jelly could taste so good. What are these purple berries?"

Mike chuckled. "Good old Montana huckleberries. They're small, but delicious. Grizzlies love 'em."

She stopped chewing and met his gaze, surprised that he would bring up the subject of bears, considering what one had done to him. "How do you know that?"

"I've learned a lot more about grizzlies than I knew before I was attacked by one. Curious about the odds of what happened to me happening to me, I suppose."

"Pretty small, huh?"

"Infinitesimal. Unless you're gutting an elk you've shot. There've been a couple of attacks on hunters in that situation, where the bear smelled blood and came looking. But no one's been killed by a grizzly in years."

"What happened to the bear that attacked you? Is it still out there?"

Mike shook his head. "It was wounded by a poacher and had to be put down. My sister-in-law, who's part of a Montana team that deals with grizzly attacks, tracked it down and shot it."

Joanna was too astonished at the thought of a woman confronting an enormous grizzly, a bear that had attacked and overwhelmed a man Mike's size, to say anything.

Mike dried his hands and filled his coffee cup before

joining her at the table. "What's your plan when the snow stops?"

Joanna was flustered by Mike's question. "I don't have a plan."

"But you'll be moving along."

He said it as a statement, rather than a question. Joanna wondered why Mike was in such a hurry to get rid of her. Likely, he valued his privacy. "If I can find a job, I might stick around in Whitefish." Joanna hadn't known where she would end up when she'd started running. She'd simply kept going north. This was as good a place as any to stop. At least for a while.

"So who are you running from?" he asked.

Joanna started at the question, which seemed to come out of nowhere. She felt alarmed and exposed. What had Daisy told him while she was asleep? She opened her mouth to say, "You have no right to ask that," but bit back the words at the last instant. She supposed she owed Mike Sullivan some explanation for how she'd ended up stranded on the highway in the middle of a Montana blizzard.

She opened her mouth a second time to name J.T. and decided that wasn't a good idea. If Daisy hadn't already told Mike his name, which she apparently hadn't, the less said about J.T., the better. "Who he was doesn't matter," she said at last. "He's someone I've put behind me."

"Did you report him to the police?"

"What?"

He gestured toward the bruise on her cheek. "For hitting you."

Joanna put a hand on the spot, which was still a little

swollen and tender. "No. He has tentacles that reach deep into local politics and government. I suspect the police would be more likely to tell him where I am than to arrest him."

"So he didn't want you to go." Again, he made it a statement rather than a question.

"No," she admitted.

He took a sip of his coffee, then focused his gaze on her. "It took a lot of guts to do what you did. But it was the right move."

"How can you know that?" she asked, more aware of his size, now that he was sitting so close.

"You and your daughter are still alive."

Joanna wanted to deny that the situation was that desperate, or would ever have gotten to a point where her life was in danger, but honestly, she wasn't sure what J.T. might have done to her, or Daisy, if she'd stayed.

"How do you know so much about things like this?" she asked.

"A Navy buddy of mine had PTSD that sent him into uncontrolled rages. I did what I could—reported his behavior and urged his wife to leave until he got counseling—but before anybody could do anything, he'd killed her. Now she's dead, and he's spending the rest of his life in prison."

"I'm sorry," she said.

"I'm just glad you got out. It doesn't look like you took much with you."

Joanna shot him a wan smile. "A little more than the clothes on our backs. But not much."

"There are resources in town for women who need assistance. When the storm lets up, I'll take you there, if you want."

Joanna shook her head. "I couldn't go to one of those places."

"Why not? That's what they're for."

"It would be admitting . . ."

"What?"

"That I was a fool."

"We all need a hand now and then. Besides, it doesn't look like you have too many options. Unless there's someone where you came from who can bail you out."

Joanna crossed her arms defensively. "My grandfather gave us what he could, and there isn't much of that left, but going to a shelter would be admitting defeat."

He lifted a dark brow. "And you're not down and out yet?"

Her chin came up. "Not by a long shot."

"I like your attitude," he said, a grin growing on his face.

Joanna flinched as the grin tortured the flesh around his mouth, making her aware, for the first time since they'd begun talking, of the damage the grizzly had done.

In an instant, his grin was gone, his chair scraped back, and he headed for the living room.

She rose to follow him, not sure whether he'd seen her horror at his ruined face, or whether this was the way he always ended a conversation. "Where are you going?" she called after him.

"I need to get some more firewood."

"Can I help?"

"You've done enough," he said abruptly.

Her heart wrenched when she realized that he'd seen her revulsion—and been hurt by it.

The door opened and closed with a *whoosh* of cold air and snowflakes, and he was gone.

Chapter 7

Mike grabbed his coat, hat, and gloves, and bolted from the house into the bitter cold, his feelings in a jumble. He could have picked up an armload of wood and returned to the house, but he wasn't ready to go back inside and face Joanna. Instead, he tromped through the deep snow to the shed where he kept his ax. He'd pretty much promised Daisy a Christmas tree. Now was as good a time as any to get her one. He hadn't walked far into the forest when he found the perfect silver spruce and set to work cutting it down.

Mike had discovered that chopping wood was a safe way to disperse the anger and resentment that often built up inside him. The repetitive swing of the ax, and the *thunk* as it bit into frozen wood, also gave him time to think. Unfortunately, his thoughts headed in an uncomfortable direction.

There was a moment this morning when Joanna looked me in the eye and saw only me, not these godawful scars. It felt good. And I couldn't take my eyes off her. How does a woman wake up looking that beautiful? I hate the comparison, but it really is a case of Beauty and the Beast.

He'd been enjoying their conversation by the fire, pleased by Joanna's willingness to share her feelings. He'd felt blindsided when she'd grimaced at his disfiguring grin. In a millisecond, her features had become neutral again, but that stark reminder of who he was, and always would be, had launched him out of his seat and out of the room.

Watch yourself, Mike. Don't ever, ever forget how you look. Just because Joanna isn't running from you in horror, don't be thinking she would consider any sort of relationship with you.

Relationship? Where had that word come from? He'd known this woman and her daughter for less than twenty-four hours. Nevertheless, Mike imagined himself as part of a family that included the three of them, having hot chocolate by the fire, laughing at the breakfast table, loving each other and caring for each other. He even imagined that fairy tale ending, a few more children with Joanna, and all of them living happily ever after.

Daisy had already captured his heart and would always hold a special place there. Joanna reminded him of himself, wounded and seeking a dark hole to crawl into. He could easily see himself providing a pair of strong arms to hold her close and keep her safe from harm.

Mike stood back as the spruce fell with a *crump* of scattering snow and the startled flight of an owl from a nearby pine. He slung the ax over his shoulder, took a good hold of the trunk, and began dragging Daisy's Christmas tree back to the house through the snow.

Giving him more time to think.

What if . . .?

Mike shook his head and made a growling sound. He had to stop fantasizing. In a day or two, when the storm was over, Joanna and Daisy would be gone from his life. He'd grown accustomed to living alone. He'd faced the fact that, like the proverbial lone wolf, he would never have a mate. He would never be a husband. He would never be a father.

Tears welled unexpectedly, and one fell onto his cheek. He had no free hand to swipe it away, and it froze there. He hated these moments, when unwelcome emotions gripped him by the throat. He'd made a good life for himself. He was fine. He didn't need a woman in his life. Or children.

Like hell you don't.

What if there were a way to get Joanna and Daisy to stay? Daisy had already accepted him as he was. If Joanna spent more time with him, maybe she would become accustomed to his face.

Not flinching doesn't mean she doesn't notice the damage. Are you telling me you think she could ignore your appearance every morning over the breakfast table? Even if she could, what about the horrified reactions of other people to your looks? Is she supposed to ignore those, too?

She would if she loved me.

How are you going to get her to stick around long enough to fall in love with you? Come to think of it, how are you going to get her to fall in love with you?

He had no idea. Not one.

Mike stopped at the woodshed to put away his ax and knock together a tree stand for the spruce, before tramping back to the house. He hadn't solved any of the issues that worried him, just raised a few more that didn't seem to have any answers.

Except, I know I want this woman and her child in my life.

So what was he going to do about it? Before his accident, Mike had been careful to make sure his sexual partners knew he wasn't ready for marriage and kids, so his encounters had been brief and mutually satisfying. Until Joanna had appeared, he'd never met a woman he thought he might want to be with the rest of his life.

Which meant he had no experience courting a woman.

He could use some advice from Rye on the subject. His brother had fallen in love at first sight, then lost the love of his life, before finally finding Vick, the two of them falling in love again, and ending up a happy family. But Mike had no phone service, and no way to get to the ranch house where Rye and Vick lived. If he didn't want to lose Joanna and Daisy, he was going to have to figure out what to do all by himself.

When Mike stepped inside carrying the tree, he found mother and daughter sitting by the fire. As he set down the tree and slipped his gloves into his pocket, Daisy jumped up and raced toward him, her eyes alight with joy. "You found a Christmas tree!"

"Sure did." He dropped his coat and hat on the rack inside the door, controlling the contorted grin that wanted to spread across his face at her excitement.

Daisy followed him as he carried the tree to an empty corner of the living room, not too close to the fire, and set it down. She ran her hand across the branches, then sniffed them.

"It's a *real* tree!"

"Of course. I just cut it down."

"Where are the decorations?" Daisy asked, looking up at him expectantly. "Can I help put them on the tree?"

"I think there might be some in the top of the bedroom closet. I'll have to see what I can find."

Joanna had joined Daisy beside the tree. She shot a look sideways at Mike and said, "Thank you. She's been worried that Santa won't be able to find her here if there's no Christmas tree."

"She told me," Mike admitted.

"How kind you are," she said softly.

Mike felt the tension in his shoulders ease. "I should be thanking Daisy." He gently ruffled the little girl's blond curls, many of which had slipped out of the braids overnight.

"What did I do?" Daisy asked.

"Reminded me that Christmas is a time for celebration."

"Uh-huh," Daisy said. "'Cause the baby Jesus was born on Christmas and the three Wise Men followed the star and the angels came and camels and donkeys and the Little Drummer Boy." She stopped long enough to take a breath and continued, "And Santa Claus comes down the chimney and puts presents for good little girls and boys under the tree, and now he'll know to come here and bring presents for me!"

Mike chuckled at her exuberance. He'd forgotten how much fun Christmas could be with a young child. His brother had always invited him to spend Christmas morning with Vick and their sons, Cody and Tommy, and their twin girls, Sophie and Stephanie, but it was too painful to be there and see what he would never have.

Besides, whenever he went to his brother's home for dinner or a special occasion, Vick tried to set him up with a woman. The prospective girlfriend always took one look at his face, where the scars drew his mouth down on one side so he looked perpetually angry, and made an excuse to leave as quickly as she could.

"I better go see about those decorations," Mike said.

Daisy tugged on his shirtsleeve. "Can I come with you?"

"I'll come, too, if it's all right" Joanna said. "To help carry things."

"Sure." Mike had forgotten about the clutter he'd left in his bedroom. Two chest drawers remained half open, with an undershirt hanging out of one. An empty beer bottle sat on the bedside table, along with a handful of change. The sheets were mussed, and magazines and books were strewn around the rug beside the bed. Not to mention the dust on every surface.

"I wasn't expecting company," he said, his face heating with embarrassment. His bedroom at home had always been a mess, but he'd argued to his mother that it was "his mess," and as long as he was willing to live with it, she should let him be. She had. Now he wished his mother had browbeaten him into better habits. He was very much aware of Joanna observing the chaos.

Her eyes crinkled and two endearing dimples appeared as she laughed and said, "I can tell there's no woman in your life."

Mike saw the moment she realized her gaffe. Of course

there was no woman in his life. He was a monster.

"I mean . . ." She met his gaze, looking him in the eye, avoiding the rest of his face with obvious effort. "I suppose it's sexist to say so, but I haven't met too many men who care much for housekeeping. Not that women care for it either. Most of us just grew up being responsible for it."

It was so cold he could see his breath, which was coming in puffs rapid enough to reveal his agitation. He turned away from her and said, "Let's just get the decorations and get back to the fire."

He pulled boxes from the top of the closet and dumped them on his unmade bed until he located his sister-in-law's decorations at the back. "Here they are."

He handed Joanna a balled up string of lights, then gave Daisy the star for the top of the tree, before retrieving a large cardboard box full of ornaments. "That's everything."

He followed Daisy and Joanna back to the living room, setting the box of ornaments near the tree.

"Can I put the star on the tree now?" Daisy asked.

"The star goes on last." Mike shot a self-conscious look at Joanna. "It's sort of a family tradition."

"That makes perfect sense," Joanna said. She held up the tangle of lights. "And since I've heard it's best to put the lights on first, I guess we better untangle these."

She'd *heard*? Hadn't she done this before? Mike wondered.

Joanna sat on the couch and patted the place beside her, indicating that Mike should sit there. He joined her, and Daisy leaned against his knee, watching carefully to make sure they did it right.

There was a great deal of laughter, his and Joanna's hands tangling as they unknotted the lights, before they finally got the string organized. Once they did, he started to put the lights on.

"Wait! Shouldn't we check first to make sure the lights all work?" Joanna asked.

"Great idea. If we had electricity," Mike said.

Joanna laughed. "I completely forgot."

Mike drew in a breath as her eyes crinkled in that way he found so attractive and the dimples appeared again. He took a mental snapshot, in case this was the only Christmas they ever spent together.

Mike let Joanna and Daisy put the balls on the limbs, Joanna at the top, Daisy at the bottom. When all the balls were on the tree, he held Daisy up so she could set the star on top.

"There," Daisy said with satisfaction. "All done."

Joanna crossed to stand beside him as he held Daisy against his chest, and the three of them admired the tree.

"I wish we could see it all lit up," Joanna said wistfully.

Mike felt a chill of alarm. Joanna had made it sound like she wasn't going to be around long enough for the electricity to come back on.

And that was when he had a brilliant, desperate idea.

Chapter 8

Joanna's throat ached as she stared at the Christmas tree. The three of them had decorated it the way she'd always imagined a family would. It was a new and wonderful experience. Her father hadn't believed in Christmas. Her mother had raised her alone after her father abandoned them, and although her mom would have loved to celebrate the holiday, she couldn't afford the time or money for a tree. Or presents to put under it.

Joanna had hoped J.T. would provide the Christmas experience for Daisy that had been missing in her own youth, but J.T. had arranged to have his condo professionally decorated, depriving the three of them of that joy. Christmas was the least of Joanna's disappointments where J.T. was concerned. It had been hard to stay in love with him when she saw how he acted toward Daisy.

J.T. had never spontaneously picked Daisy up and held her close, the way Mike often did. J.T. had never listened to

Daisy to discover what she wanted, and then gone out of his way to get it for her, as Mike had done with the Christmas tree. And where J.T. was concerned, the less he saw or heard of Daisy, the better.

Joanna laid a hand on Mike's sleeve and felt his muscles tense beneath the wool. She realized it was the first time she'd voluntarily touched him. She shouldn't have been surprised at the muscle and sinew she felt beneath her fingertips, but it made her more aware that he was a man. A very strong man.

Who's caring. And gentle.

It was foolish to be frightened of Mike Sullivan. His ravaged face, enormous height, and powerful body were deceiving. He certainly was capable of breaking her neck, and likely would have by now, if he'd actually been the dangerous beast everyone saw when they looked at him. But she was getting to know a man she suspected very few people had met since his encounter with the grizzly, one who was far more likely to protect her and Daisy than harm them.

Joanna shuddered at the thought of what it must be like to look into the mirror and see that horrific face staring back at you. She'd seen signs of bitterness in Mike, but it hadn't kept him from being generous. It hadn't kept him from being considerate. It hadn't kept him from being kind.

The word *kind* kept leaping to mind whenever she thought of Mike, and she wondered why it seemed so important to her.

Maybe because you've experienced so little kindness in your life. Maybe because you can't imagine such a caring man treating you badly. Or hitting you. Or abandoning you.

Was Mike's thoughtfulness the real deal? Or an illusion? Anyone could be nice for a day or two, but would his actions stand the test of time?

Joanna kept her eyes focused on the upper half of Mike's face, but her gaze was inevitably drawn to the scar that pulled his mouth down on one side. She tried to imagine herself kissing Mike. As she surveyed his lips, she realized there was nothing wrong with them. They were beautifully shaped, with a surprisingly delicate bow at the top. A scar crossed the right edge of his mouth and kept his cheek from coming up when he smiled.

She took quick, furtive glances at each of the raised scars on his face, lowering her gaze each time so she wouldn't get caught. She noted where one ran into the hairline at his right temple. Another crossed down through his right brow. Yet another ran down his left check, disappeared into his beard, and reappeared on his neck, before finally disappearing beneath his wool collar. Which made her wonder what his naked chest might look like. It was a very broad and muscular chest.

It took her a moment to realize that Mike had noticed her examining him and was looking at her with an odd expression. She flushed and said the first thing that came into her head to avoid acknowledging what she'd done. "I can't tell you how grateful I am that you found a tree for Daisy."

"I didn't do it just for her. I did it for you. And for me, if I'm being perfectly honest. I'd forgotten how much I love Christmas." He hesitated, then continued, "Which brings me to something I've been meaning to discuss."

Joanna realized Mike had put his hand over hers on his sleeve. She waited to feel threatened by the action, but all she felt was . . . comforted.

"Look," he said, "I've got an extra bedroom with a bunk bed that can be separated into two twins." He smiled, drawing his mouth down farther on one side.

Because she knew the distortion was coming, and because she'd analyzed what caused it, she wasn't surprised by it and managed not to recoil from it.

"You and Daisy are welcome to stay as long as you like," he finished in a rush.

Joanna was stunned by his offer, desperate enough to take advantage of it, and at the same time, leery of it. "We couldn't impose on you like that."

He cut off her objection with a wave of his hand, ending their physical connection. "It sounds to me like you don't have a lot of options. Right now, neither one of us has a working vehicle. Once this storm winds down, I can borrow my brother's truck and take you into town to hunt for a job, while Harry fixes our pickups. Waitresses are always in short supply in Whitefish."

"I'll need to find someone to take care of Daisy."

"I'm sure my sister-in-law would lend a hand."

"Thank you, but—"

"Then it's settled," he interrupted. "You'll stay here with me until you have the funds you need to move on."

Joanna wasn't sure what to say. So she said nothing. But saying nothing was saying yes. She'd opened her mouth to refuse Mike's offer, when the Christmas tree lights suddenly came on, turning the tree into something warm and cheery that made the cabin, with its log walls and crackling fireplace, feel achingly like home.

"Mommy! The lights came on!" Daisy clapped her hands in delight. She turned to Mike and said, "Mike, look! The lights came on!"

"They sure did," Mike said.

A moment too soon. If the electricity had come on a second later, Joanna would already have told Mike Sullivan that she and Daisy had to move on. That she had no intention of asking him to take care of them for one more day, never mind depending on him for the indefinite future. But she'd remained silent, and the moment had passed. Now, looking at the colored lights reflected in her daughter's shining eyes, she didn't have the heart to drag Daisy back out into the cold.

A sharp knock on the door startled Joanna, and she turned to Mike for reassurance.

He made a face that she thought was meant to be wry and said, "That'll be my brother. I imagine Vick sent him here to check up on me. Rye's likely seen my pickup rammed against a tree and will be worried whether I'm all right." He said all this as he made his way to the door. He opened it and dragged his brother inside, shutting out the lashing snow.

Joanna watched as Mike's brother embraced him, hugging him tight. He let him go and stomped his feet, releasing the snow that covered him to his knees onto the rug inside the door.

"You son of a bitch! When we couldn't reach you, Vick said I'd better come make sure you hadn't frozen your ass off. When I saw your truck, I wasn't sure what I'd find."

"Watch your mouth," Mike said, shooting a look at Daisy. "I've got company."

"You've got what?"

Joanna watched Rye's jaw drop as he took in the lighted Christmas tree, four-year-old Daisy standing beside it, and finally, Joanna.

Rye's face split into a grin as his gaze returned to Mike. "Well, well, little brother. I see you've been busy."

Joanna watched Mike flush, which made his scars stand out white against his pinkened skin. As the brothers stepped farther into the room, Joanna observed that, except for the color of their eyes, the two brothers must have looked alike before Mike's accident. They had similar noses and thick dark eyebrows, and Rye had the same bow in his upper lip. Because of Mike's beard, it was impossible to tell whether he and Rye had the same jawline.

Daisy crossed to stand at Mike's side, staring up at Mike's brother with her head tilted like an inquisitive little bird.

"This is Joanna Henderson and her daughter, Daisy," Mike said, picking up Daisy.

"We have a Christmas tree," Daisy said. "The 'lectricity came back, and the lights are really pretty."

"I see that," Rye said, turning to Mike with his brows raised.

"Nice to meet you," Joanna said, walking forward with her hand outstretched to greet Mike's brother. "Mike rescued us when my car stalled on the side of the road."

"We're going to live here," Daisy volunteered.

Joanna shook her head in disbelief and muffled an embarrassed laugh with her hand. She'd forgotten how good Daisy was at listening and then repeating what she'd heard.

"When did all this happen?" Rye asked, turning to

Mike.

"Joanna and Daisy have been here since late yesterday. I offered them the second bedroom today, and Joanna accepted."

Joanna saw that Rye was now looking at her with suspicion in his moss-green eyes. Why would a woman agree to live with a strange man after knowing him for less than twenty-four hours? And Mike was not simply a stranger, he was a man deeply scarred in body and soul. A man his brother obviously believed needed protecting from predatory females like Joanna.

She was spared an explanation when Mike said, "Some guy has been giving Joanna a hard time. She's been on the road for a while and needs a place to stay while she gets back on her feet."

Joanna felt her face heating at such plain speaking, but the suspicion left Rye's eyes, replaced with compassion. He turned to Mike and said, "I'd better give Vick a call and let her know you're still alive."

"My cell died, and my electricity has been out," Mike explained.

"How did you run your truck into a tree?" Rye asked.

"Oh, that was the kitten's fault."

"There's a kitten?" Rye said incredulously, searching the room.

"Uh-huh," Daisy said, and then continued in a single breath, "Her name is Mittens and she sits in Mike's lap and purrs really loud."

This time, Rye's eyebrows nearly hit his hairline. "A cat, Mike? Really?"

"It's growing on me," Mike said gruffly.

Rye turned to Joanna and said, "Let me know if my wife and I can help you with anything."

"I volunteered Vick to babysit for Daisy while Joanna looks for a job," Mike said.

"If it's too much trouble—" Joanna began.

"No trouble at all," Rye said. He turned back to Mike and asked, "Does the fact that you have a tree up mean you'll be joining us this year for Christmas?"

"That depends on Joanna," Mike said, shooting a glance in her direction.

"What? Why is that?" Joanna asked.

"I don't know how you feel about spending the day with strangers," Mike said.

Joanna focused her gaze on Rye and said, "We wouldn't want to intrude on a family gathering."

"I've always believed that, where Christmas is concerned, the more the merrier," Rye said.

Since Joanna agreed with him she smiled and said, "Then we'll be glad to join you."

"I guess that settles it," Rye said, slapping Mike on the shoulder.

With a sudden flurry of snowflakes, he was gone.

Joanna turned to Mike, a look of astonishment on her face. "Is he always like that?"

"Like what? Bossy? Telling me how I should live my life? Yeah. Pretty much."

"I'm surprised you weren't already planning to spend Christmas with your family," she said, taking Daisy from him and perching her daughter on her hip.

"Rye wasn't kidding when he said 'the more the merrier.' Half the town shows up at the ranch house for punch and cookies before the day is done. It's chaotic and noisy as hell. I'd rather sit by the fire at home and enjoy the peace and quiet."

Joanna met his gaze and wasn't sure what she was seeing. Suddenly, she knew: a man lying to save his pride. She pictured Mike at his brother's home, unable to hide his face with a scarf or his hands with gloves, pretending he didn't notice all the surreptitious glances in his direction. Pretending he didn't see the reactions to his destroyed face in people's eyes.

Mike Sullivan doesn't enjoy being alone. He tells himself that untruth because he doesn't think he has any other choice if he wants to protect himself from being hurt. He's had no one to stand by his side throughout a day filled with curious neighbors and make it clear to everyone that he's just a nice, normal guy, nothing more and nothing less.

Except, now, thanks to her and Daisy, he did.

Chapter 9

Mike didn't know what had come over him, offering Joanna and Daisy a place to live. For a while. Until she moved on. He only knew he couldn't let this woman and her child leave. Not yet. Not until he knew they would be safe.

Rye's first reaction to hearing what he'd done was pretty much what Mike had expected. With a single look, Rye had made it clear that he believed Mike was leaping off a pretty damn steep cliff without looking and, most likely, would end up getting hurt.

But Rye wasn't the one who'd spent the past five years alone. Having Joanna and Daisy here had pointed out to Mike with startling clarity exactly what he'd been missing.

"If Rye was able to get here, the roads are driveable," Mike said. "I better call Harry and have him come tow our pickups and give us a ride into town," Mike said, grabbing his cell and plugging in the charger. "He usually loans clients one of his beaters while he does repairs, so we'll have wheels until we get at least one of our vehicles back."

"Is the storm over?" Joanna asked, staring out the window at the falling snow.

"Pretty much," Mike said. "If we waited for perfect weather in Montana, we'd never leave the house."

Joanna smiled, and he felt his heart jump. And realized his brother was right in his guess about the danger he foresaw. Mike was way out on a ledge, and if he wasn't careful, he could very easily fall . . . in love.

Then he realized what he was about to do. He was going into Whitefish in broad daylight. Even with a scarf to cover most of his face, Joanna would see firsthand the reactions of other people to his scars. He glanced sideways at her, wondering if she would be embarrassed to be seen with him. And whether it would occur to her that the kind of reactions he got, the revulsion and horror, would happen whenever he went out in public.

For a moment, he considered staying at the cabin and sending Joanna into town with Harry by herself. He could offer to stay home and babysit for Daisy. Except, Joanna didn't know her way around town, or who to see for a job.

He would have to go.

Maybe that was for the best. If Joanna was going to be scared away by other people's opinions of him, it would be better if it happened now, rather than later. Maybe it would provide the reality check he needed to keep his feelings for her from growing any stronger.

Mike arranged for Harry to take Joanna's truck to his garage first. Once he'd done that, he'd make a second trip to Mike's place to tow his pickup. When Harry arrived at the cabin to pick them up at mid-morning, with Mike's truck already attached to the tow truck, he reminded Mike of everyone's favorite grandpa, with his scraggly beard, fluffy white hair topped by a Christmassy red-and-green knitted wool cap, and a substantial paunch that ballooned under his coveralls and oil-stained fleece coat.

Sitting in the front bench seat of the tow truck as they drove back to Whitefish, Mike watched Daisy, who was belted onto Joanna's lap between him and Harry, charm the old man as easily as she'd charmed him.

"We have a Christmas tree but there was no 'lectricity so the lights didn't work and then they did and Mike held me up so I could put the star on top."

Harry shot a look at Mike with eyes that twinkled merrily and said to Daisy, "Uh-huh."

Which was all the encouragement Daisy needed to continue, "And Mike nailed three funny socks up by the fire."

Joanna was less forthcoming, but she smiled gratefully at Harry when he offered Joanna his daughter's cell number so Daisy and his five grandkids could get together over the holiday to play. Mike was relieved to hear Joanna tell Harry that when her pickup was repaired, he should call her at Mike's cabin.

Mike figured she was using his home number because she didn't want someone pinging for her cell number to locate her, like the guy she'd left behind. But Harry apparently attributed another meaning to her statement—that she and Mike were a couple.

He shot Mike a questioning look.

Mike ignored it. He wasn't about to offer any explanation for how Joanna and Daisy had ended up moving in. Harry was an incurable gossip, and Mike didn't want folks around town making assumptions that might not turn out to be true. Even so, he was pretty sure the fact that Mike Sullivan had a woman and a little girl living with him at his cabin would find its way around Whitefish before the day was out.

Mike wasn't sure what he thought about that. In a practical sense, it might keep a few of the single guys in town from making a move on Joanna if they thought she already had a relationship with him.

Except, she didn't.

You aren't being fair to Joanna by keeping her anything-but-romantic relationship with you a secret. On the other hand, how much of her past does she want anyone to know? What can you tell Harry that he hasn't already figured out for himself?

Mike justified his silence with the argument that he'd said as much to Rye as he felt comfortable revealing, and the rest of Joanna's story was hers to tell.

When they reached Harry's garage, the old man offered one of his rattletraps to Mike, then turned to Joanna and said, "Do you need a separate car?"

"How long will it take to fix my truck?" she asked.

"Depends on whether I can find the parts," Harry replied. "It's a pretty old model."

She shot Mike a troubled look before she said, "I think I'll be okay riding with Mike for a while. Let me know what you find out."

"Sure," Harry said as he handed a set of keys to Mike. "It's the green pickup behind the garage. Needs gas."

"Of course it does," Mike said.

Harry laughed. He was notorious for refusing to fill the gas tank of his beaters, leaving that job to the folks who borrowed his cars.

Mike took Joanna to the Safeway in town, which had good food at good prices, rather than to Markus Foods, the well-known local grocery on the edge of town that catered to folks heading up toward Big Mountain, where supplies cost a little more. Better she shouldn't be seen there anyway. If anyone she knew was going to show up in Whitefish, that was where they'd end up shopping.

Before his injuries, Mike had often gone grocery shopping with his nephew, so he had some inkling of how a four-and-a-half-year-old might react to all the different foods displayed on the shelves. But, once again, Daisy surprised him.

She didn't make a peep, didn't point at a single item, didn't beg or cajole her mother for anything special.

It was unnatural.

The longer Mike and Joanna walked through the store, Joanna putting a lot more healthy foods in their cart than had been in his house over the past five years, the more concerned he got.

Daisy was walking alongside the cart, and he finally touched her shoulder and asked, "Is there something you'd especially like to eat, Daisy?"

Daisy glanced up at him briefly, then focused her gaze on her feet and answered, "No."

"Nothing?" he persisted.

She shot a look at her mother, who said, "It's all right, Daisy. If there's something you'd like to have, you can tell

Mike."

With a sinking feeling in the pit of his stomach, Mike realized what he was seeing. Daisy had apparently been taught to stay silent while shopping. Why? In order not to upset the sort of man who displayed his temper by destroying a child's doll. Mike felt his face flush with anger. What had J.T. threatened to make Daisy so obedient? What awful lesson had she learned from him at a grocery store?

Mike had never hated another human being before. He didn't like the way it made him feel. Hot. Edgy. Frustrated. Like he wanted to punch something. He hoped he met J.T. someday. He might just teach the son of a bitch a few lessons of his own.

Chapter 10

Joanna was surprised at how easy it was to get a job. In fact, it seemed a little unreal how it happened.

A young man with a bushy blond beard, who was dressed in jeans, hiking boots, and a North Face jacket, left his grocery basket sitting at the meat counter and trotted over to Mike, his hand outstretched. She could tell Mike felt self-conscious greeting the guy, but he stuck out his hand anyway.

The man openly surveyed Mike, then said, "You're not looking too bad for a man who had his face ripped off by a grizzly."

Joanna couldn't believe what she'd heard.

To her amazement, Mike shot back, "It beats that ugly mug of yours."

The stranger laughed. "How are you, buddy? Haven't seen you at Loula's in forever."

"Been busy," Mike said.

"Got a piece of Flathead cherry pie with your name

on it," the man said. "Why don't you stop by after you finish shopping?"

"I . . . uh . . ." Mike floundered.

Joanna realized Mike could give as good as he got with a friend, but he was clearly uncomfortable with the idea of sitting down in a cafe filled with strangers.

At that moment, Daisy reached for Mike's hand, looked up at him, and announced, "Cherry's my favorite. Can we go, Mike?"

Joanna could tell Mike wanted to say no. Before he could, the stranger asked, "Who you got there?"

Daisy was still clinging to Mike's hand, so he lifted it slightly and said, "This is Daisy." He gestured to Joanna and said, "And this is her mother, Joanna. They're friends of mine."

Friends? Joanna thought. They were barely acquaintances. But it saved a lot of explanations.

Mike turned to Joanna and said, "Dave is the cook at Loula's Cafe."

"Hold it right there, buddy. Don't be telling your girl I'm an ordinary cook," Dave corrected. "I'm the *chef* at Loula's."

"Point taken," Mike said. "When I left Montana to become a Navy SEAL, Dave headed to culinary school in the South and became a *chef*."

"Somehow we both ended up back here in Whitefish," Dave finished with a grin. "Nice to meet you, Joanna."

Joanna took the hand he offered and shook it. "Nice to meet you, too."

"How 'bout it, Mike?" Dave said. "Gonna come eat

some pie? Although I don't know who's gonna serve it. I just lost my best waitress. Some elk hunter up from Texas in the fall came in for a piece of huckleberry pie, took one look at her, and fell head over heels. Came back yesterday to make a Christmas proposal and off she went to meet his family."

"This is your lucky day," Mike said. "Joanna's looking for a job."

"Really?" Dave said enthusiastically. "You're hired."

Joanna was still frozen in place at the mention of a hunter in town from Texas, fearing he might have a connection to J.T., who'd also hunted elk. It took her a moment to realize what had just happened. "Wait," she said with a startled laugh. "You don't know anything about me."

"Mike recommended you," Dave said. "That's good enough for me. When can you start?"

Joanna stared at him in disbelief. Was this really happening? She'd done some waitressing as a teenager but nothing since, and she didn't want to disappoint Mike's friend. But she needed a job, and it didn't make sense to turn this one down. "When do you need me?"

"As far as I'm concerned, you can put on an apron and serve Mike his cherry pie. We can fill out the paperwork at the end of the day. Gotta go, Mike. See the three of you in a bit?"

"You bet," Mike replied.

Dave returned to his cart and disappeared around a corner.

Joanna thrust both hands into her hair, turned to Mike and asked, "What just happened?"

"You got a job at one of the best restaurants in town. Loula's is nationally known for its pies, especially their huckleberry and Flathead cherry."

A half hour later, Joanna ended up serving Mike and Daisy their Flathead cherry pie, so-called because the famously delicious cherries were grown locally along Flathead Lake. The cafe was busy, and she was relieved to see how quickly her waitressing skills came back to her. The diners included both locals and tourists, but they were uniformly friendly.

That didn't mean they disregarded Mike's ravaged features. Inside the cafe, he'd been obliged to take off his coat, gloves, hat, and scarf, revealing the full damage done by the bear. Most people sneaked glances when they thought Mike wasn't looking, unable to avoid ogling him the way they might have slowed down to rubberneck at an accident on the road. Others kept their gazes focused anywhere but on him, which made it even more obvious that they were avoiding what they found it difficult to look at.

Joanna admired the way Mike ignored them, although he wasn't unaffected by their scrutiny. She noticed how the hand that wasn't holding his fork was fisted on his knee under the table. And how a muscle jerked in his jaw when a mother shushed her child's cry of fright.

And she understood with sudden clarity why Mike had been so reluctant to come here. This must happen to him whenever he tried to be "just one of the crowd." She could see what it cost him to indulge in the simple joy of eating a slice of cherry pie in Loula's Cafe. None of these people perceived the generous-hearted soul who'd taken in a stray woman and her daughter. All they saw was a bearded brute.

Her heart ached for him.

Despite the stares, he sat at the table smiling and chatting with Daisy as though he didn't have a care in the world, wearing a stoic outer shell that protected him from the pain he must feel when people recoiled from him. It didn't hurt her opinion of him to know that he'd come here—fully aware of what would happen—for her sake.

She saw how surprised Mike was when someone he knew smiled and waved at him from across the room. That made two people today who'd known him in the past—three, if you counted Harry—who'd ignored his scars. And surprised him by doing it.

But she understood why he avoided being in the company of strangers. They gawked. They gasped. And they made him aware of the blighted features he would carry with him the rest of his life.

Joanna met Mike's gaze from across the room and caught the look of longing he didn't have time to hide.

Why, he's attracted to me! I don't know why that should surprise me. I'm attracted to him, too. Which sounds odd when I say it to myself, because no one would think you'd be attracted to a face like Mike's. But he has a body I'm itching to touch and wonderful blue eyes and a mouth I've thought about kissing.

Joanna realized she was daydreaming when a customer lifted a hand to get her attention, holding up a coffee cup.

When she'd filled the customer's cup, she noticed Mike was gesturing for her to join him. She crossed with the pot of coffee in hand and asked, "Would you like a little more coffee with your pie?"

"I need to go by the ranch and see whether Rye needs help putting out hay for the cattle. How would you feel if I took Daisy by the house and introduced her to Rye and Vick's four-year-old twins, Sophie and Stephanie?"

Joanna was torn. She wanted to meet Mike's sister-in-law before she left Daisy with her, but she couldn't very well leave early her first day on the job. She had no doubt Daisy would enjoy playing with other girls her age, and since both she and Mike had to work, Mike's suggestion made sense. She felt sure Mike wouldn't leave Daisy in any situation that made her daughter uncomfortable. "That sounds like a good idea," she said at last.

When she saw the relaxation in Mike's shoulders, Joanna was glad she'd decided to trust him with Daisy. "Does that sound okay to you, Daisy?" she asked her daughter.

Daisy said, "Uh-huh," but her eyes didn't agree with her mouth. Her daughter looked anything but happy.

Joanna's stomach clenched. "Are you sure, Daisy?" Although she had no idea what she would do with her daughter if she didn't want to go with Mike.

Daisy repeated her unconvincing, "Uh-huh," but then reached for Mike's hand.

Joanna realized that Daisy was having as much trouble with this unexpected separation as she was, but her daughter's trust in Mike was comforting. "All right, then," Joanna said, bending and kissing her daughter's forehead. "Have a good time. I'll see you soon."

"Daisy and I will be back at the end of your shift to pick you up," Mike said, rising and helping Daisy on with her coat.

There was an awkward moment when, if they'd been an actual couple, Joanna and Mike would have embraced or kissed. Mike reached out awkwardly to pat her on the shoulder. "Don't worry about Daisy. I'll take good care of her."

"I know you will."

Then Joanna did something that surprised both her and Mike. She stood on tiptoe and kissed his cheek, the cheek with the scar that made his mouth slant downward on one side. She felt her face flushing and noticed Mike's face was ruddy as well.

"Thank you, Mike," she said, looking into his eyes as she spoke. "For everything."

She wasn't sure what she would have said next, or what he might have said, because a patron entering the cafe called out, "I need a slice of that famous huckleberry pie!" and she hurried away to get it.

Chapter 11

Once he got outside, Mike put a hand to his cheek where Joanna had kissed him and felt the raised scar. She must have felt it, too, with her lips. He'd never been so surprised in his life. Not just that she'd kissed him, but that she'd done it in a room full of strangers who must have wondered how she could bring herself to get that close to him.

He'd felt sure Joanna would be put off by all the horrified, terrified, and pitying looks he'd been getting from the folks in Loula's. It had been an agony sitting there pretending it didn't matter what they thought. He'd come there for Joanna's sake but had ended up learning something he hadn't expected.

He didn't have to live his life in the dark. He didn't have to live his life away from people.

Mike had been confused by Dave's reaction—or rather, his total lack of reaction—to his scarred face. And what about Jack Stanley, from the hardware store, who'd greeted him at the cafe with a smile and a wave? Did the blemishes really not matter? It had felt strange to meet old friends and be treated like the attack had never happened. Which made Mike wonder whether he'd been doing his friends a disservice. He'd never given them a chance to reject him. He'd rejected them first.

What if they wouldn't have turned away from him? What if they missed him as much as he missed them? Sitting in Loula's with a piece of cherry pie had given him a lot of food for thought.

Mike belted Daisy into the front seat of Harry's old beater because he didn't have a child's carseat—he'd have to get one of those—and it didn't have an airbag that could injure her if it went off. He'd been expecting her to make a fuss about leaving her mother and going off with him, but she not only didn't complain, she didn't make a peep until they were halfway to the Rafter S.

Daisy was staring at her hands, which were clasped in her lap, when she said, "What if those girls don't like me?"

"What makes you think they won't?" Mike asked.

She looked up at him and said in a small voice, "I'm a trouble and a trial."

"Who told you something like that?" Mike said, although he had a pretty good idea.

"I was playing with Roxie and knocked over a lamp and J.T. said I'm 'corgable and should be sent away to board school, but Mommy said no, absolutely not, never."

"It's board*ing* school," Mike said. "And you're not *incorrigible,* you're a great kid. Your mom is right. You belong at home."

"Do you really think they'll like me?" Daisy asked.

"Sophie and Stephanie are going to love playing with you," Mike said. "That is, if you like dolls and Legos. And they have a dog named Rusty that's fun to play with, except you have to be careful, or he'll lick you all over."

He was rewarded with a small smile.

"It's okay if he licks me," Daisy said, smoothing her hands over her tiny skirt. "I like dogs."

Which reminded him that one of the first things Daisy had told him was how someone had poisoned her dog. He was getting a pretty ugly picture of this J.T. character.

Fortunately, they arrived at the ranch before Daisy's jitters could get any worse. Mike came around the truck to unbelt her and picked her up to carry her inside. He was surprised when she clutched him around the neck and hid her face against his throat. The Daisy he knew was anything but shy.

The back door wasn't locked, and he let himself in and called out, "Anybody home?" The ranch house was warm and had an ancient Coldspot refrigerator that hummed pretty much all the time.

He tried to set Daisy down but she clutched him tighter, so he left her where she was. He heard screeches of laughter coming from the back of the house and then pounding footsteps on the hardwood floor as the four-year-old twins came running down the hall yelling in unison, "Hi, Uncle Mike!"

The twins stopped cold in the doorway.

Vick stopped right behind them.

"Hello, Vick. Hi, girls," Mike said, keeping his features neutral, since his face looked less intimidating if he didn't smile. He felt Daisy lift her head from his shoulder and glance at the newcomers.

"You must be Daisy," Vick said with a welcoming smile.

To Mike's surprise, Daisy quickly turned her face away and pressed her nose against his neck again. Mike went down on one knee, which forced Daisy's feet onto the floor, but she wouldn't let go. He held on to her with one arm, while he extended the other to embrace the twins—who didn't come tumbling toward him as they had the last time he'd seen them.

Then he realized just how long ago that had been. Which meant they hadn't seen his face for . . . Could it really be two months?

"Give Uncle Mike a hug," Vick urged, putting a hand on each girl's shoulder and urging them forward. When they resisted, she shot Mike an apologetic look.

"Who's that with him?" Stephanie asked her mother, remaining close to her twin.

It dawned on Mike that he'd overestimated the effect of his ugliness yet again. It might not be his damaged face Sophie and Stephanie were reluctant to approach. It might be Daisy.

"This is Daisy," Mike said, putting both hands on her waist to turn her toward the two blond-headed girls, who had pigtails similar to Daisy's and wore matching denim coveralls. "She's staying at my house with her mom. I thought you girls might like to play together this afternoon."

There was a moment when Mike was sure Daisy was going to turn her back on the twins and run for the hills, figuratively, anyway. He could feel the tension in her small body, the expectation of rejection, the fear of it in her narrow, bunched shoulders. The bubbly little girl he knew was suddenly mute.

He wasn't sure what would have happened if Rusty hadn't barged into the kitchen. He headed straight for Daisy, tail wagging furiously, and began licking her face.

Mike held his breath until he heard Daisy's laugh ring out. A moment later, she released her hold on Mike to hug the large, shaggy mutt around the neck.

The dog's acceptance of Daisy, and Daisy's acceptance of Rusty's effusive greeting, ended whatever restraint had kept the twins from greeting him. They ran to Mike, babbling about how Santa was going to come soon and bring them presents because they'd been good little girls and an elf moved around the house every night all by himself and they had to search for him until they found him each morning.

He waited with bated breath for the moment the twins addressed Daisy, or she addressed them. He didn't care which one spoke first. He was on tenterhooks hoping it would happen before an awkward silence fell.

"You have an elf in your house?" Daisy asked the twins, her blue eyes wide with wonder.

"Uh-huh," Sophie said. "He's got bells on his shoes."

"We try to hear them when he moves at night, but we're always asleep," Stephanie added.

"Can I see him?" Daisy said.

"Sure," the twins said together.

Mike met Vick's gaze, his eyes filled with gratitude for the kindheartedness she'd taught her girls. Each girl took one of Daisy's hands and started toward the living room.

He'd thanked Vick and was on his way out the kitchen

door when Daisy, breathless from running all the way back from the living room, jerked the hem of his coat and said, "Are you coming back?"

"Of course I am." Mike's heart nearly broke when he saw the panic in her eyes. "We have to go pick up your mom in a little while. I'm just going to put out some hay for the cattle, so they have something to eat."

"You're sure you're coming back?" she asked, meeting his gaze with eyes far too distrustful for a four-year-old.

Mike went down on his haunches, so he could look Daisy in the eye. "If you need anything, Vick can call me. I'm right outside."

"Okay, Mike," she said reluctantly. "If you say so."

"I say so. Now scoot. Go have fun!" He aimed her toward the living room and gave her a pat on the rump.

The hardest thing Mike had ever had to do was open the kitchen door and walk out, leaving that anxious little girl behind. Daisy didn't know it yet, but she was going to learn that, when Mike Sullivan made a promise, he kept it.

Chapter 12

The instant Joanna tumbled into the passenger's seat of Harry's loaner after work, she felt an electricity between herself and Mike that hadn't been there before she'd kissed his cheek. She shot a glance in Mike's direction, but he had his gaze firmly fixed on the road as he drove them out of town. Fortunately, Joanna only had to ask, "Did you have a good time today?" and Daisy filled what would have been an awkward silence.

"Sophie and Stephanie look exactly alike!" Daisy burbled. "Except Sophie has a tiny little scar on her chin right here." Daisy pointed to the center of her chin. "They're really nice and they have lots of dolls and *two* older brothers." She held up two fingers. "We all built a snowman and they have a dog named Rusty and he licked my face and, oh, yeah, they have the very best thing of all."

Joanna brushed the bangs from Daisy's brow, reassuring herself that her daughter was here and safe after an afternoon spent apart, and asked, "What's the very best thing of all?"

"An elf!"

Joanna shot a confused look at Mike. "An elf?"

Before Mike could explain, Daisy continued, "He has bells on his shoes and he moves around at night when you're asleep and you have to find him every morning. Can we get one?"

Joanna had no idea what Daisy was talking about. "We can discuss it later."

Daisy's lips pouted. "That means no."

"No, it doesn't," Joanna protested. "It means I need time to find out a little bit more about it."

Daisy wasn't that patient. "Mike, can I have an elf?"

Mike shot Joanna a wry smile and said, "I'll talk to your mom, and we'll let you know."

Joanna was grateful for Mike's deference, making the decision hers, and at the same time, irritated that Daisy had turned to him rather than accept her answer. She wondered if she was just grouchy because she was frazzled from serving up two thousand pieces of pie. Joanna laughed to herself. Well, somewhere between twenty and two hundred, anyway.

Daisy constantly chattered through dinner, saving Joanna from having to talk to Mike about the elephant in the room.

That kiss.

It was nothing. The simple touch of her lips to his cheek.

It was more than that. It meant something.

What was Mike thinking? Should she say something? Or wait for him to mention it? Or pretend it never happened? *It happened.*

The fact that Mike had been trying to catch her gaze all through dinner made it clear that he certainly hadn't forgotten about it. But there was no way she could say anything—they could discuss anything—until Daisy was in bed.

However, Daisy was so keyed up Joanna realized she was going to have trouble getting her daughter to sleep. A bath helped. A little. By the time Daisy was in pajamas and in bed waiting for a story, Joanna was running on fumes. She'd forgotten how exhausting it was to spend hours on her feet.

Mike had unstacked the twin beds, separating them with an end table that held a lamp in the shape of an Air Force jet. Joanna sat down on the edge of Daisy's bunk, which was covered with a bedspread full of toy cars, and read a chapter from *Winnie-the-Pooh*, one of the books Vick had sent home with Daisy.

She stopped reading when Daisy's eyes began to droop. She set the book aside and pulled up the covers, but Daisy's eyes flew open and she said, "I forgot to say my prayers."

"I forgot, too" Joanna said. "I'm listening now."

Joanna loved her daughter, but she wished Daisy didn't have quite so many people for God to bless. The list now included everyone she'd met that day. When Daisy finished, she seemed as wide awake as Joanna was sleepy.

"I wanta kiss Mike good night," Daisy said.

Joanna felt a spurt of jealousy. And realized how foolish that was. She raised her voice and called, "Mike, would you come in here, please?"

Mike appeared in the doorway a few moments later, a questioning look on his face, meeting her gaze for the first time since they'd returned to the house. There was a whole world of possibility in those eyes. Joanna felt butterflies take flight in her stomach as he asked, "Do you need something, Joanna?"

She thought: *I need your strong arms around me, holding me close.*

She said: "Daisy would like you to kiss her good night."

"Come closer," Daisy said.

Mike sat down gingerly on the opposite side of the bunk from Joanna.

Joanna had mixed emotions as she watched Daisy grasp the front of Mike's shirt and tug until he leaned close enough for her to kiss her forehead, each cheek, and finally, lightly touch her lips to his mouth, in exactly the way Joanna kissed her daughter each night at bedtime.

"Good night, Mike," Daisy said.

"Good night, sweetie," Mike said.

When Mike stood and met Joanna's gaze, his eyes were bright with tears. "I'll be waiting for you in the living room," he said as he headed for the door.

Waiting for me? To do what? To say what?

Joanna felt an unaccustomed lump in her throat. She couldn't remember a man in her life who'd been vulnerable enough to let her see that sort of emotion. Her veins hummed with expectation as she listened to his footsteps heading down the hall.

"Now you kiss me good night, Mommy," Daisy said.

She kissed Daisy, who finally, at long last, sighed, turned onto her side, and closed her eyes. Joanna sat beside her for a long time, unwilling to examine her feelings. Afraid to examine them.

Joanna had spent most of her life mistrusting men. What was so different about Mike Sullivan? How had he so quickly gotten past all the barriers she'd set up to protect herself from getting hurt yet again?

You foolish, foolish woman. You want to believe in the fairy tale. You want to believe that a man can care enough about you to keep his promises. You want to believe that, if a man loves you, he won't hurt you.

All men are liars. You can't let down your guard. You can't trust Mike Sullivan. You can't trust any man.

As she walked down the hall, Joanna heard the warning clanging in her brain like a fire alarm at grammar school, but the moment she entered the living room, it flew completely out of her head.

Mike had lit a crackling fire, and the room was toasty warm. He'd stacked pillows on the floor and used a blanket to make a nest facing the fire.

"Make yourself comfortable," he said.

Once she'd dropped onto the floor, he handed her a cup of cocoa topped with melting marshmallows and said, "I thought you might want something hot and sweet to drink."

Mike settled himself on the floor cross-legged beside her. She realized he'd taken off his shoes and that one of his socks had a hole in the toe.

While they sipped their cocoa, they sat in a silence that was surprisingly comfortable. The silence was comfortable.

Her proximity to Mike was not.

She could feel the heat of his big body. Hear him breathe. See the bulge of muscle in his thighs through his jeans. She lifted her gaze to avoid what else might be bulging and ended up looking right into his eyes.

Which was a big mistake. She felt . . . antsy. She wanted something, but she didn't know what. Or maybe she did know and wasn't happy with the knowledge of what it was she wanted.

"Mike . . . I . . ." she began.

"Why did you kiss me?"

Well. That was taking the bull by the horns. Joanna shrugged. "I don't know."

"Nobody's kissed me in five years."

Joanna was appalled. Not his mother or sister-in-law or some woman he knew? Or even his nieces or nephews? "No one?"

Mike shook his head. "My fault, really. Since I got out of the hospital, I've never allowed anyone to touch my face. Except you. And now Daisy. I'm not sure what I would have done today if you hadn't surprised me like that."

"I'm sorry if—"

"I'm not," Mike interrupted. "Having you here has opened my eyes to a lot of things."

When he paused, Joanna lifted a questioning brow.

He took a deep breath and let it out before he continued, "I've shut out everyone who ever tried to get past the wall I put up when I came home from the hospital and saw what I looked like in the mirror. Not just the mirror on the wall, but the horrified faces reflecting back to me what I'd become.

"I've avoided my friends for years. I was shocked when I realized today that a lot of people I used to know don't care what my face looks like. I'm the only one who cares.

"I understand that was a kiss of gratitude, nothing more. I don't expect anything from you. I just wanted to tell you that I'm glad your car got stuck. I'm glad you decided to stay."

Joanna hadn't been aware of setting down her cup. Or leaning back against the pillows. Or even closing her eyes as she listened to Mike, but she awoke when he scooped her up off the floor, blanket and all. She slid an arm around his neck, her fingers skimming the silky hair at his nape. She kept her eyes closed as he carried her down the hall and settled her on her bed.

She was aware of his hesitation after he pulled the blankets up over her shoulders and wondered if he was thinking about kissing her. Joanna felt disappointed when he rose from her side, turned out the light, and left the room without any further contact.

The next morning, she awoke to a shriek of excitement from her daughter and raced into the living room to find out what had happened. Daisy's face was split into a grin that ran from ear to ear. She followed her daughter's finger as it pointed upward.

An elf had appeared on the mantel.

Mike leaned against the fireplace, a cup of coffee in hand, his mouth horribly distorted as he grinned back at her daughter.

That was the moment Joanna fell suddenly and inexplicably in love with him.

Chapter 13

During the twelve days since Joanna had discussed that simple kiss on the cheek with Mike—and despite an almost palpable sexual tension between them—he'd made sure they were rarely in each other's company.

Mike left the house in his repaired truck each day before breakfast and came home just in time to tuck Daisy into bed and kiss her good night. Afterward, he sat on the opposite end of the couch from Joanna in front of a crackling fire while they each drank a cup of hot chocolate, asking her about her day but sharing nothing of his own. Then he moved Daisy's elf and retired to his bedroom. Alone.

He'd remained an enigma, a puzzle she couldn't seem to solve.

Joanna suspected that Mike was as scared of caring for her as she was of caring for him. Despite her strong attraction to him, she was afraid of being disappointed. Again. He seemed to believe that no woman could fall in love with a man who looked like him. And he wasn't about to give her a chance to break his heart.

But the more Mike dodged any chance of intimacy between them, the more determined Joanna became to break through the invisible wall he'd put between them. What if Mike was that steadfast man she'd always believed was out there waiting to love her? Now that she'd found him, wasn't it worth the risk of finding out for sure?

And there was no time to lose. Harry had called today to announce that her pickup was finally fixed. Now that Joanna had a job and her truck was driveable, there was no reason for her to continue living with Mike. And she was convinced that, if she left without telling him how she felt, he would cut her and Daisy out of his life.

Joanna gritted her teeth. The war for Mike's heart was on. Somehow, she had to break through his iron reserve and convince him that what he thought was impossible had, in fact, already happened. She wanted to know him better. She wanted to be held in his arms. She wanted . . .

"Mike!"

Joanna was jerked from her reverie by Daisy's shout of joy as she raced toward Mike, who'd just come through the door. Joanna rose to greet him. She was fighting for her future and Daisy's—and Mike's. Her battle plans had been made, and the first skirmish was about to begin.

When Mike came through the door, Daisy wasn't in bed waiting for him to kiss her good night. Joanna hadn't even fed Daisy supper, let alone bathed her and gotten her into pajamas. Joanna had set the table, cooked dinner, and then waited for Mike to arrive.

Hi, there, sweetie," Mike said, smiling with a joy she could see was equal to Daisy's, lifting the little girl high enough into the air to cause her to squeal with delight. "What are you still doing up?"

As usual, Daisy spoke without periods at the end of her sentences. "We waited for you and I helped peel potatoes and we're having ice cream for dessert."

Joanna met Mike's startled look in her direction with a smile of welcome. "We got tired of eating all by ourselves. I hope you're hungry."

"As a horse," Mike admitted. "Isn't it a little late for Daisy—"

"She's as hungry as you are," Joanna interrupted. "You'll have to get home a little earlier in the future."

Mike's brow furrowed, pulling his scars into a knot.

Joanna pretended she didn't see his consternation. His days of avoiding the two of them were over. She had a couple more sorties up her sleeve to convince Mike that she and Daisy weren't going to fade into the background anymore.

"My truck is ready to be picked up," she said as she took the meat loaf out of the oven and set it on the table. She joined Mike and Daisy, who were already seated, and said, "I only have to work a half day tomorrow, so it'll be convenient to drop off the loaner and retrieve my grampa's truck. Daisy and I are going to church with your family tomorrow evening. Are you coming, too?"

"I don't go to church," Mike said, keeping his eyes on his plate.

Joanna had learned from Vick that church was another

thing Mike had given up after the grizzly attack. Before she could pursue the subject, Mike turned to answer a question from Daisy. Joanna listened patiently while they carried on a conversation that was mostly an excited Daisy telling Mike about her day and Mike responding, "Uh-huh," and "I see," and "That sounds like fun." She couldn't help comparing his keen attention to Daisy to the way J.T. had so constantly shushed her daughter. Which only made Joanna more firmly resolved to break through Mike's defenses.

As she set a bowl of ice cream in front of her daughter, Joanna said, "Daisy and I would love for you to take us to the Christmas Eve service. Wouldn't we Daisy?"

That was playing dirty pool, but Joanna didn't care.

Right on cue Daisy said, "I could sit on your lap. I get to hold a candle but I have to be careful 'cause I could catch fire." She vigorously stirred her ice cream, then stopped, stared right into Mike's eyes and said, "Pretty please, will you come?" Daisy had learned that "pretty please" business from Joanna.

Joanna watched Mike's resistance melt like the puddle Daisy was making of her chocolate ice cream.

He shot Joanna a helpless look, then turned to Daisy and said, "Sure, sweetie."

"Yaaaaay!"

Mike hunched his shoulders in a sham attempt to protect his ears from Daisy's yell and laughed. He turned to Joanna and said, "She's pretty wound up. We better get her into the tub, or she's never going to get to sleep tonight."

"Take your pick," Joanna said. "Dishes or Daisy."

"Daisy," he said, rising and grabbing Daisy out of her

chair, his armed wrapped around her like a football, making her giggle as he headed down the hall to the bathroom.

Joanna hurried to stack the dishes in the dishwasher so she could join Mike. She needn't have rushed. He was sitting on the floor beside the tub, which was full of bubbles, reading Daisy a chapter from *Winnie-the-Pooh* while she played with a rubber duck and a toy boat.

When Joanna showed up in the doorway he said, "I thought we could kill two birds with one stone. Bath and bedtime story at the same time."

"Good idea." Joanna slid onto the tiny spot left on the floor in front of the tub, picked up a cloth and soap, and began washing Daisy. Both she and Daisy laughed when Mike read Piglet's part in a hilarious falsetto.

When Mike saw she was done bathing Daisy, he closed the book and said, "I'll finish this tomorrow, sweetie."

"Tomorrow's Christmas Eve," Daisy reminded him. "Santa's going to come while I'm sleeping and bring presents for everyone."

She chattered with Mike—rather, chattered to Mike—while Joanna toweled her dry and dressed her in pajamas. Mike stayed in Daisy's doorway as she said her prayers and came to her when she held out her arms to him without Daisy having to say a word. Once she'd kissed him good night, he left.

Joanna tucked Daisy in one last time, turning out the light, even though she begged for another story. "The sooner you go to sleep," she said, "the sooner tomorrow will come."

That was enough incentive for Daisy to turn over and say, "Good night, Mommy."

Joanna closed the bedroom door and headed into the living room, expecting to find Mike sitting on the couch holding a cup of hot chocolate, with another cup waiting for her on the coffee table.

Mike was there, all right. But he was standing by the fireplace with his arms crossed over his chest. There was no cocoa in sight.

"What's going on, Joanna?"

Joanna settled onto the couch as though this were just another ordinary night. "I don't know what you mean."

"We aren't one happy family. There's you and Daisy. And there's me. Eating dinner together and bathing Daisy together and going to church together isn't going to change that."

Joanna rose from her seat and took two steps around the coffee table to confront him. "What will?"

He appeared momentarily flummoxed, especially since she'd made a point of getting into his space. "Will what?"

"What will bring us closer? I'd like to know." She reached out and laid a hand on his folded arms and felt the muscles go rigid. She looked up at him, her heart in her eyes and said, "Don't you want to know me better?"

She watched a crease form between his eyes before he finally said, "It would be a waste of time. I don't see you hanging around for long, now that you have a job. I don't want . . ."

When he hesitated, she finished the sentence for him. "To get hurt."

"No. I don't."

"I just want to know you better."

His eyes flared with some emotion.

It took Joanna a moment to realize what it was. *Desire.* Hot, no holds barred, take her any way he could get her passion. She drew in a sharp breath as blood thrummed through her veins and pooled in her belly. She couldn't remember the last time she'd felt such swift and certain arousal.

"I want you," he said in a guttural voice. "Have since the moment I first laid eyes on you. Safest thing for both of us is for me to spend as little time as possible anywhere near you."

Joanna had a decision to make and no time to think about it. "I want you, too," she said in a quiet voice. "What are we going to do about it?"

Chapter 14

Mike had his arms wrapped around Joanna faster than she could blink an eye and lowered his head to capture her mouth with his. This moment was everything he'd ever dreamed when he thought of Joanna. Something stopped him when his lips were only a breath away from hers.

What am I doing? Can this be real?

He lifted his head and searched Joanna's eyes, looking for the truth. Did she want him, a man to whom she was attracted, as improbable as that seemed? Or did she merely feel grateful to him? More bluntly, was she offering him what his SEAL buddies would have called a "mercy fuck," something you gave to a poor soul for whom you felt sorry?

There was nothing in her blue eyes to reveal the answers he sought, but she leaned trustingly against him, and her hands had slid into the hair at his nape. She didn't seem reluctant. Her body was warm and yielding, her breasts pillowed against his chest.

"You want this?" he said in a gruff voice. Unable to ask what he really meant: *You want me?*

In answer, she framed his cheeks with her palms and said, "Why don't you kiss me and find out?"

Despite his fear that this was all a dream, that Joanna would disappear if he didn't hold her tight with both hands, Mike had never been so gentle with a woman. His lungs were bursting with air he was afraid to exhale as their lips met.

It felt right. It felt good. It felt . . . perfect.

He heard a sigh of satisfaction from her and released the painful breath that had been trapped inside him. Mike had always enjoyed kissing, and he'd done enough of it to do it well. He loved the tastes and textures of Joanna's mouth, and he was in no hurry to move on. He relished the anticipation they were building for what would come later. He held her close and let their bodies get acquainted, feeling the growing warmth of breast and hip and thigh undulating together, as their tongues danced to an ageless tune all their own.

He was surprised when Joanna broke their connection and followed her retreating mouth with his until she put a hand on his chest and whispered an urgent, "Mike."

She was panting, her breathing erratic, and her eyes had a misty look that suggested confusion.

He loosened his grasp, and she put enough space between them that he noticed the absence of her heat, the loss of her supple curves.

So. She'd chickened out, he thought bitterly. When push came to shove, she couldn't make herself go through with it. He supposed he had his answer to those earlier questions.

"My legs are like noodles," she said breathlessly, not meeting his gaze because of what it took him a moment to realize was shyness. "I wondered if we could continue this in your bedroom."

When she looked up at him, he knew she must be seeing his face at its very worst, which is to say, the way it looked when he was grinning from ear to ear. She laughed in surprise when he scooped her into his arms and said, "All you needed to do was ask."

When Joanna's feet touched the floor in his bedroom, Mike put his big hands on either side of her face and kissed her reverently. She was so small. And he was so big. He was afraid he'd hurt her. Or scare her. He felt hot all over as the blood surged through his body, his shaft engorged and throbbing long before he knew Joanna could possibly be ready for him.

The need—*the want*—inside him was overpowering, extending from his center like the petals of a flower. He wanted to undress her slowly, revealing what he'd only imagined. He wanted her as aroused as he was. He wanted the night to go on without end. He wanted her to have a dozen orgasms. Well, maybe not that many, but more than one for sure. He wanted her like he'd never wanted anything or anyone in his entire life.

Joanna followed his lead as he toed off his cowboy boots, leaving them both wearing jeans and socks. When Joanna started to pull her socks off he said, "The floor's cold. Leave them on."

He was so careful removing her buttoned-up blouse that he was clumsy. She was having equal difficulty releasing the buttons on his wool shirt. He nudged her hand away, took hold of the two sides of his shirt and yanked. Buttons were still pinging across the wood floor as he ripped it off, along with the long john shirt beneath it, leaving him half naked. He shivered as the cold air hit his flesh.

She laughed at him for being in such a hurry, her face beautiful in its joy as she scraped her blouse off over her head, not bothering with her own buttons, either, then reached back to undo her bra.

"Let me," he said in a husky voice.

She dropped her hands as he unhooked the bra and pulled it off her arms before looking down to see her small, firm breasts with their pink, rosebud nipples.

He wondered if he'd ever seen a sunrise half so beautiful. Or a snowfall. He shook his head at his foolishness.

He reached out to gently cup the weight of her breast in his hand and brushed his thumb across the nipple, hearing her gasp and watching it tighten into a bud before his eyes.

He met her gaze again before leaning down to take the nipple in his mouth and gently suckle. He felt her hand on his head like a blessing.

Mike heard a yelp that reminded him of an animal caught in a trap and raised his head, listening alertly. He heard glass break, and then a child's cry of terror.

Mike grabbed Joanna's shirt from the floor, threw it at her, and yelled, "Get dressed!"

He grabbed a baseball bat from under the bed, turned the doorknob, and swore when he remembered he'd locked the door so Daisy couldn't walk in on them. He finally threw it open, and raced for Daisy's bedroom.

Mike had grown attached to Joanna's daughter, but he hadn't realized how strong his feelings were until he thought Daisy might be in danger. His gut was tied in knots, and his heart was rocketing in his chest as he slammed open Daisy's bedroom door and punched on the overhead light. He gasped when Mittens streaked past his ankle and scampered down the hall toward the kitchen.

"Damned cat!" he muttered as his stomach slewed sideways.

It took a moment for his eyes to adjust and take in the scene before him. The intruder he'd expected to find was nowhere to be seen. Daisy sat huddled with her back against the headboard, the covers pulled up to her neck, her face hidden on her knees. The glass of water that had been on the bedside table lay broken on the floor. He set the bat down beside the door and tiptoed around the broken glass in his stocking feet to the other side of the bed.

"Daisy?" he said in his softest voice, as he sat down beside her. When she didn't respond, he laid a hand on her shoulder. At his touch, she made a cry of protest and her body quivered. He took his hand away and knotted his helpless fingers in his lap. "Sweetie, what's wrong? What can I do to help?"

Where was Joanna? he wondered. What was taking her so long? Her daughter needed her.

Daisy lifted her face, and his stomach clenched at the fear he saw in her eyes as she searched the room, peering into the shadows in the corners. "I saw him," she whispered.

"Who?" he asked.

"J.T. He was here."

Mike wondered if it was possible the man had been in the house, in this room, but there hadn't been time for him to escape before Mike had shown up at the closed door. "It was just a bad dream, sweetie."

"He wants Mommy, but not me. I don't want to go to board school," she sobbed.

Mike didn't resist the urge to comfort her. He lifted Daisy out from under the covers and tucked her close to his heart. His chest felt seared where her hot tears dropped onto his naked flesh. "You're safe, sweetie," he said, his voice a croak because his throat was knotted with anger toward a man he'd never met.

He heard a whimper and turned to find Joanna standing in the doorway, her eyes stark, a hand to her mouth to cut off the sound. He met her gaze and said, "No one's taking you anywhere you don't want to go. I promise you that."

Chapter 15

Joanna wanted to cross the room, hug her child close, and never let go. But she was afraid her daughter would be frightened by the way her mother's body was shaking. Joanna had to cross her arms to keep herself from splintering into a million pieces.

Daisy had never had a nightmare. This was something new, another remnant of their lives with J.T. As Joanna stared at her daughter, held protectively in Mike's arms, she acknowledged that this was a nightmare, all right. But it was hers, not Daisy's. She was the one who'd stayed too long with a man who didn't value her or her daughter. Joanna could do nothing about her decisions in the past, but she could make wiser choices in the future.

She wanted to trust her gut, which told her Mike was a good guy. Everything he'd done in the two weeks since she'd met him had encouraged her to like him and trust him. He clearly adored Daisy. Tonight, she'd come very close to sharing herself with him in a way that would have deepened their connection. She was the one who'd encouraged such intimacy. Mike had been more cautious.

What did he know that she didn't? What reservations of his had she overcome that perhaps she should have respected?

Joanna stepped around the broken glass and sat on the end of the bed next to Mike, reaching out to brush a sweaty lock of hair away from her daughter's cheek. Joanna found it significant that Daisy was content to rest in Mike's arms, rather than reaching for her mother. If she hadn't been so glad Mike was there to protect them both from the bogeyman, she might have been jealous.

"Would you mind holding Daisy while I clean up this broken glass?" she said. "I'm the only one wearing shoes." She'd stopped long enough in the bedroom to slip on her cowboy boots, not sure whether she might need their extra bulk to kick some intruder where it would hurt the most.

"No problem," Mike replied.

Joanna's heart pounded as she made her way down the hall to the kitchen to retrieve a broom and dustpan. Once she was in the kitchen, where no one could see her, she shook her arms to try and get the shivering to stop. On her way back to Daisy's room, she made a detour to lock the front door, which Mike always left open. It helped her nerves a little, but she was still jittery as she carefully swept up the broken glass.

"I'll just dump this in the kitchen," she said when she was done, grateful to get out of the room before her unsteady knees collapsed, and she landed in a heap on the floor.

When she returned for a second time, she found Mike sitting where she'd left him. He was caressing Daisy's hair, while the little girl was patting his bare shoulder. Who was comforting whom? she wondered. "I made a trip around the room with Daisy while you were gone," Mike said. "Just to make sure there's no one hiding in the closet or under the bed."

"I locked the front door, so no one can get in," Joanna said. She sat down beside Mike and laid a comforting hand on Daisy's shoulder. She was relieved when her daughter didn't flinch. In her softest voice she said, "Time to go back to bed, sweetheart."

Her daughter stared at her with wide, anxious eyes, then hid her face against Mike's naked chest. "I'm scared."

Joanna's belly clenched as she imagined how terrified Daisy must have been by whatever nightmare had woken her to still be afraid. Even Mike's efforts to show her daughter there was no one lurking in the shadows hadn't helped to assuage her child's fear. Joanna didn't know what to say. She settled for something that would take Daisy's mind in another direction. "Tomorrow is Christmas Eve," she reminded her daughter. "We have a busy day planned."

Daisy lifted her head and looked at Joanna, then up at Mike. "Will you stay with me till I fall asleep?"

Joanna met Mike's gaze and saw his jerky nod. "We'll both be right here," she promised. Joanna rose and turned on the lamp beside Daisy's bed, then crossed the room and turned off the overhead light, watching as Mike settled Daisy under the covers. He plumped up her pillow and pulled the covers up under her arms, then tucked his way down around her sides and under her feet, ending with, "Snug as a bug in a rug."

Joanna was surprised to see Daisy smile at him. She hoped that meant her daughter was finally putting the nightmare behind her. That this was a one-time thing. That it would never happen again.

Joanna crossed the room and sat on the opposite side of the bed from Mike. Because she needed physical touch to reassure herself that her child was all right, Joanna tucked a strand of hair behind Daisy's ear.

Mike reached for a book and began reading, but he didn't get very far before Daisy's eyes drifted closed and her rosebud mouth slid slightly open. When it was clear Daisy was asleep, Mike met Joanna's gaze and whispered, "Should I leave the bedside light on or turn it off?"

"Leave it on," Joanna whispered back as she stood. "That way, if she wakes up again, she'll be able to see there's no one in the shadows."

Mike nodded, then rose and crossed around the bed to her.

Joanna realized his arms were open wide, and she walked right into them, letting Mike comfort her, just as he'd comforted her daughter.

"You're trembling," he said.

In fact, the shaking had never stopped. "I'm scared, too," she admitted. "What if J.T. finds me? Finds us?"

"I meant what I said. I won't let anybody harm you or Daisy. Not while there's a breath left in my body."

His arms tightened around her, and she squeaked and then laughed and said, "Keep that up, and there won't be a breath left in mine."

He shot her a rueful smile, then shifted her so he could settle his arm around her shoulder. Her arm naturally slid around his waist, and they walked together, not toward the bedroom, but down the hall toward the living room. Joanna found the direction Mike had turned very telling. It seemed he wanted to take a step back as well.

He led her to the kitchen, turned on the light, and settled her in a chair at the dining table before taking a chair across from her. "We need to talk."

Joanna searched his face, listening for everything he was saying that didn't involve words, although the words he spoke weren't what she'd expected. His blue eyes were focused on hers as he reached across the table and took her hand, smoothing his thumb over the back of it.

"I was afraid this would happen," he said.

Joanna's heart sank. He wanted out. He wanted her gone. He didn't want to get involved with someone being chased by a man so awful he made her quake like a leaf in a storm.

"I love you."

Joanna's jaw dropped. "What?"

"I love you. And I love Daisy. I didn't want it to happen. I couldn't stop it. I know it's way too soon for you to be thinking about caring for anyone, let alone a man like me."

"Stop right there!" Joanna said sharply, pulling her hand free.

He looked startled.

"A man like you?" she said, arching an angry brow. "Too soon to fall in love with a thoughtful, caring man? You must not think much of me to believe that."

He flushed. "I meant—"

"I know what you meant. Your face is scarred. People seeing you for the first time are going to stare. But I've learned a bit about the man who lives inside that scratched-up body. He's a good man, a man any woman would be proud to love."

Joanna didn't admit that she loved him, because even if she said the words, she didn't think he was ready to believe them. It was hard enough to believe them herself.

"It's time for me to find a place of my own," she said. Joanna noticed the downward twist of Mike's mouth and continued, "If I stay here, we're going to end up in bed again." She shot him a wry smile. "Not that I would mind if that happened. But we need space to find out whether what's been growing between us is real or simply the result of living in such close proximity."

"My feelings aren't going to change, no matter how much distance you put between us," he said.

"The problem is my feelings," she admitted. "I don't want to make another mistake, Mike. I owe it to myself, and to Daisy, to choose the right man to share my life. I haven't been very good at that in the past. I need to be certain that you're that man."

Mike looked away. He had to clear his throat before he asked, "When are you moving out?"

"After the holiday. I don't want to spoil Christmas for Daisy. She's already worried that Santa won't find her here, despite everything you've done to reassure her." She smiled to ease the sting of her decision, but when Mike finally met her gaze, the unhappiness she saw in his eyes nearly broke her heart.

"I'll miss you," he said. "Both of you."

"It's not as though we'll be going far," she said, anxious to soften the sting of what he apparently perceived as a rebuff. "I'll find someplace in town, and you'll have plenty of opportunities to see Daisy."

"I'd like that. What about seeing you? How is that going to work?"

"There's this thing called dating."

His face contorted in a wry smile. "Dating. Yeah, I've heard of it."

She laid a hand on his bare forearm, wanting one last touch before they went their separate ways, and felt the warm flesh tense beneath her fingertips. In a soft voice, she reminded him, "You can always stop by Loula's and see me. We can share a piece of Flathead cherry pie."

Joanna waited for the wretched look of sadness to leave his face. But it was still there as they rose from the table and headed to their separate bedrooms.

Chapter 16

Joanna found it encouraging that Mike joined her and Daisy for breakfast the next morning, rather than running off to work as he had the previous two weeks. In fact, he and Daisy were at the table before her, and Mike had cooked a pot of oatmeal that was waiting to be dished up from the stove. The kitten was eating its breakfast from a bowl near the sink.

As Joanna served everyone, she was relieved to see that, despite Daisy's nightmare, her daughter was her normal chatty self. Joanna exchanged a look with Mike, whose blue eyes crinkled with laughter at Daisy's prattle.

"I found the elf, Mommy. He was hiding on top of the refrigerator." Daisy pointed to where the elf sat. "Can Mike take me to see Sophie and Stephanie today?"

Before Joanna could point out that it wasn't polite to be asking Mike for favors, he said, "I'd be happy to take her. I have some chores to do on the ranch this morning anyway."

Joanna realized she couldn't be more indebted to Mike than she already was and conceded, "That would be a big help. After I work my half day, I'll be exchanging Harry's loaner for my grandfather's pickup. I can come pick her up afterward."

"Or you could drop off Harry's loaner, leave your pickup where it is until after the holidays, and Daisy and I could come into town to get you."

Mike held her gaze for a moment, letting her digest the ramifications of what he'd suggested. Then, as though her answer wouldn't contain a wealth of subtle meanings, he picked up a carton of milk from the table and filled Daisy's glass.

If Joanna did what Mike had proposed, the three of them would have to go everywhere together over the holiday. Mike was making it plain that he wanted to spend as much time as possible with her and Daisy before they took off. He'd already made it clear that he'd rather they didn't leave in the first place.

Joanna recalled the reverence in his eyes as he'd undressed her. The combination of tenderness and passion when he'd kissed her. The butterflies bombarding her insides as he'd suckled her breast.

All of which led her to wonder if she was being foolish moving out. Moving away from Mike. Sometimes, she felt sure it was the right thing to do. The problem was she didn't want to go. She wanted more mornings like this. Everything about it felt . . . right.

Joanna reminded herself that she had good reason to be careful. She'd made mistakes in the past. Taking a little time to get to know Mike better was a good idea. Wasn't it? For instance, she'd never seen him really mad. And they'd never had a serious argument. What if there was another, less likeable Mike lurking behind that ruined face?

She glanced sideways and saw Mike shift Daisy's bowl away from the edge of the table before tucking her daughter's napkin more firmly into her shirt under her chin.

I think what you see with Mike Sullivan is what you get, a voice inside her argued. *He's the genuine article. A good man.*

The temptation was there to throw caution to the winds, to tell Mike she'd changed her mind. To tell him she still wanted to get to know him, but she didn't need to live somewhere else to do it. She opened her mouth, but instead of speaking, she spooned in a bite of oatmeal to give herself more time to consider what made the most sense.

Her stomach was churning as she measured her choices. Leave? Or stay where she was? Travel with Mike over the holidays? Or have access to her own vehicle?

Joanna was going crazy trying to make up her mind. Two bites of oatmeal later she'd decided that, at the very least, she wanted to retrieve her grandfather's truck.

At that moment, Daisy spoke.

"I'm glad we left Texas," her daughter said. "I like it better here with Mike."

Joanna felt a tremor of alarm run through her. She hadn't anticipated resistance to the idea of moving on from Daisy. "I like it here, too," Joanna agreed. "But we can't stay with Mike forever."

"Why not?" Daisy asked.

"We need to find a home of our own," Joanna said, eyeing Mike, who was smart enough not to say anything.

"I want to live here!" Daisy said, tipping her chin up mulishly and banging her spoon in her oatmeal, sending cooked oats flying.

"Daisy, that's enough," Joanna warned, reaching out with a paper napkin to clean up the mess.

Daisy turned to Mike and said in a pleading voice, "Can I stay, Mike?"

Mike met Joanna's gaze, but he pressed his lips together to keep whatever he wanted to say from coming out.

"It's not fair to put Mike on the spot," Joanna said, as upset now herself as Daisy seemed to be.

"Don't you like me?" Daisy asked Mike, her eyes brimming with liquid hurt.

"You know I do, sweetie."

Joanna saw frustration in Mike's eyes as he focused them on her, could tell that the invitation to stay as long as they liked sat on the tip of his tongue. She almost let him speak. But that wasn't fair to him. Two adults had no business letting a four-year-old manipulate them into something other than what they'd discussed and she'd decided.

"This isn't up to Mike," Joanna said firmly. "It's up to me."

Daisy dropped her spoon, glared at Joanna, and said, "You're mean!"

Joanna felt a spurt of guilt and fought it back. She was trying to do what was best for both of them. Joanna shoved her chair back and stood. "If you're done, Daisy, it's time to go. Get your coat."

Mike shot Joanna a startled look. He'd apparently

been so engrossed in the conversation that he'd stopped eating. His bowl was still half full.

"If you're not ready to go, I can take Daisy," Joanna said, working hard to keep the edge out of her voice.

Mike stood abruptly, wiped his mouth, and threw the paper napkin on the table. "I'm done."

Joanna felt even worse for forcing Mike to leave his breakfast sitting on the table. Not that she'd eaten much of her own. Daisy's bowl wasn't empty, either. And, as everyone had jumped up from the table, Mittens had dashed out of sight, abandoning her half-full bowl as well. Not one of them had finished the meal Mike had prepared.

What had happened to their perfect morning at the breakfast table?

Daisy stood at the front door mutinous, her arms crossed, refusing to put on her coat. "I want to live here."

"I have to go to work," Joanna said, her voice sharp. She held out Daisy's coat, waiting for the little girl to put it on.

Mike teased Daisy's coat from Joanna's tight grip and said, "You go on ahead to work. I'll make sure Daisy gets where she needs to go."

Joanna was exasperated to see that, the moment Mike held out the coat to Daisy, she immediately thrust her arms into it. He knelt and zipped up the coat, then pulled the hood up over Daisy's head and tied that, before finding the mittens in her pockets and easing them onto her tiny hands.

Joanna turned to Mike and, in the calmest voice she could muster, said, "You don't need to pick me up after work. I'll meet you back here when my shift is done."

It was small satisfaction telling Mike that she didn't

need him, that she'd rather retrieve her grandfather's pick-up, so she'd have her own wheels over the holiday. Joanna turned her back on the two of them—Daisy was chatting happily with Mike—and marched out the door. She wasn't going to give her daughter—or Mike—the satisfaction of seeing how left out she felt.

Chapter 17

"You're in a foul mood."

Mike glared at his brother, who stood on the other side of the ranch's 4x4, as Mike scattered a bale of hay he'd lifted from the bed of the truck onto the snow-covered ground where a few Black Angus cattle had gathered. "What makes you say that?" he snarled.

"Oh, I don't know," Rye said. "Maybe the way you've growled your way along the entire fence line while we've been dropping hay." He leaned his elbows against the edge of the pickup bed and asked, "Do I detect a little female trouble?"

Mike grabbed the side of the pickup bed with his leather-gloved hands and hefted himself up and into it in a single powerful move, before plopping down onto a couple of the remaining bales of hay. "Are you gonna talk all day or drive?"

"Talk," Rye said, staying where he was rather than getting back behind the wheel. "How are things going with

Joanna?"

"Drop it," Mike said warningly.

"Don't think I will," Rye said, levering himself into the bed of the pickup with equal ease and sitting on a bale of hay across from Mike, his breath making clouds of fog in the cold. "Tell big brother all about it."

The last time Rye had confronted Mike like this and asked to hear what he had to say was the day Mike told his family he was moving away from the ranch to Vick's cabin. As Mike recalled it, Rye was the only one who hadn't tried to talk him out of it. He'd just listened. He hadn't judged.

"She's moving out," Mike blurted. "Right after Christmas."

Mike waited for Rye to comment, but his brother remained silent.

"I don't want her to go," Mike continued. "I love her."

He met Rye's gaze, daring his brother to point out that falling in love with a woman after knowing her for such a short time was nuts.

All Rye said was, "I see."

"That I'm an idiot?" Mike shot back.

"You've been a lot more careful than I was," Rye said in a quiet voice. "I fell in love with Vick the first moment I laid eyes on her."

"So you don't think I'm crazy?"

Rye grinned. "I didn't say that."

Mike shook his head and chuckled but sobered a moment later. He fixed his gaze on Rye and said, "What should I do?"

Instead of answering, Rye asked, "What about the little

girl, Daisy? How do you feel about having an instant family?"

"That kid is amazing. I'd love being her father."

"Then what's the problem?" Rye asked.

"Joanna just got out of a pretty nasty relationship. The bastard hit her." Mike's jaw flexed. "And he terrorized Daisy. Joanna's still shell-shocked," Mike said. "She wants to take her time before committing to anyone else. Especially so soon. She wants us to date."

"And that's a problem because . . .?" Rye asked.

"Once she moves to town, she'll have a lot more choices besides me. And they'll all be better looking."

"You think your appearance makes a difference to Joanna?"

Mike swallowed over the sudden knot in his throat. "Sometimes, I think she doesn't mind. Then I wonder how that could possibly be true. I mean . . ." He gestured toward his face.

"A woman in love won't notice those scars. Speaking of which, how does Joanna feel about you?"

"I don't know." The words were wrenched from Mike's very marrow. Joanna had dismissed his looks as unimportant and said he was a man "any woman would be proud to love." But in the next breath, she'd announced she wanted to move out. So, maybe she liked him. But that wasn't even close to the same thing as loving him.

An image of Joanna's avid gaze as they'd undressed each other rose in his mind's eye. She also desired him. But that was none of Rye's business. Besides, Mike had bedded enough women to know that love and desire didn't necessarily go hand in hand.

"Have you told Joanna how you feel?" Rye asked.

"Yeah."

"What did she say?"

Mike grimaced. "Nothing that makes any difference. Look, the sooner you get back in the cab and drive, the sooner we can dump the rest of this hay and get out of the cold."

Rye jumped down from the truck bed, but he paused and turned back to Mike. "Will we see you at church tonight?"

Mike realized he was actually looking forward to the service. He thought of how excited Daisy was and how nice it would be to stand beside Joanna and share a hymnal and how much he'd missed the joyous sound of Christmas music. "I'll be there," he said at last.

"What are you doing the rest of the day?"

Joanna had made it clear that she would come to the ranch to pick up Daisy, so Mike didn't have anywhere he had to be. He shrugged as he watched the snowflakes begin to fall, confirming that their white Christmas was going to be even whiter, and said, "I've got no plans."

"You didn't ask for my advice, but here it is. As soon as we're finished here, get yourself to Loula's, see your girl, and have a piece of Flathead cherry pie."

Mike didn't see what good it was going to do to show up at Loula's, but before he could say so, Rye was back behind the wheel. On the other hand, Rye had never steered him wrong.

The moment they were done, Mike jumped into his pickup and headed for town. With any luck, he could get there before Joanna's shift was done.

And say what? Do what? What could you possibly say

or do to change her mind about moving out?

Unfortunately, his mind remained blank during the drive into town. He'd already offered the best arguments he could come up with to keep Joanna at his cabin. Nothing had worked. But he couldn't give up. He had to keep trying. Surely, once he saw her, the right words would come to him.

The snow was coming down a lot harder by the time Mike made it to Loula's. He stepped inside and stomped his boots at the door to rid them of snow. There were no other customers, and Dave was out front wiping off one of the empty tables.

Mike took a look around and asked, "Where's Joanna?"

"You just missed her," Dave replied.

"She went home?" Mike said, his heart sinking.

Dave shook his head. "Things were slow enough that I told her to go turn in Harry's loaner and retrieve her pickup now, so she can just head out when her shift is done, before the weather gets any worse. She hasn't been gone for more than a few minutes. You want to have a piece of pie while you wait for her to get back?"

"No thanks," Mike said, ignoring Dave's startled look as he turned right around and headed back outside into what was quickly becoming another blizzard. He'd never been so happy to see the weather go to hell. The continuing snow flurries, which threatened visibility on the road, provided the perfect excuse for Joanna to leave both Harry's loaner and her grandfather's pickup at Harry's garage and let him do the driving. That would at least ensure they spent the holidays together. And every day in Joanna's company gave him another chance to win her love.

He headed to the parking lot in back of Harry's garage, where Joanna would be dropping off Harry's beater and retrieving her pickup.

Mike's heart caught in his throat when he saw Joanna struggling against the hold of a tall, slender man in a knee-length, camel-hair coat who was trying to force her into the trunk of a black Lexus. He knew immediately who it had to be. Mike's face flushed with anger as his heart pumped adrenaline. Every muscle in his body tensed for battle as he jammed on the brakes and threw open the door.

Chapter 18

"Hi, Joanna."

The blood drained from Joanna's face as she stepped out of Harry's pickup and found J.T. standing before her in the isolated parking lot behind the garage.

"You're looking better than I expected," he said. "You've certainly landed on your feet. A job. A place to live. I heard you've even found yourself some ugly fool to sink your claws into."

Joanna's heart was pumping a mile a minute, while her eyes searched for routes of escape. While she'd been parking the loaner beside her grandfather's truck, leaving the key under the mat per instructions from Harry, who was home with his family, J.T. had blocked both vehicles with a sleek black Lexus. She was caught in the narrow metal lane between the two vehicles with a cement wall behind her. Her only hope of getting away led past J.T., who loomed as large and dangerous as a riled-up grizzly.

Adrenaline surged through Joanna's body, propelled by rage and fear. "How did you find me?"

"That truck of your grandpa's is rare enough that there are only a few places where you can get parts. I figured sooner or later it would break down. Sure enough, it did. I tracked the order for parts to Whitefish. I got Harry talking about that piece of junk, said I might like to buy it, and he told me where you worked and gave me a number where I could reach you, in case you weren't at Loula's. I considered walking in and having you serve me a piece of that Montana huckleberry pie. But this seemed like a better idea.

"Especially after that fiasco last night. That kid of yours nearly took ten years off my life, screaming like that. I had the devil's own time getting out of there without getting caught."

The hairs rose on the back of Joanna's neck. "You were in Mike's house?"

J.T. sneered. "I used the phone number Harry gave me to trace the address. The front door wasn't even locked. I was looking for you when the kid saw me."

Daisy hadn't been having a nightmare. She'd actually seen J.T. If her daughter hadn't woken up, there was no telling what J.T. might have done.

"It was a stupid move," he continued, "especially when I knew you'd be coming here sooner or later. Harry told me your grandfather's pickup was ready to go, so I've been watching this place, waiting for you."

Joanna shivered with revulsion. *J.T. had been watching her?* Her chest was so constricted with dread it was hard to draw breath to speak. "Why are you here, J.T.?"

"To take you home, of course."

With horror, Joanna realized J.T. had no intention of taking Daisy along. Despite the frigid cold, her face suddenly felt hot. Her stomach knotted "I'm not going anywhere with you."

J.T. smirked.

A fury rose inside Joanna for all the times J.T. had made her feel helpless and worthless. "Get the hell away from me."

"Too late for that. You're mine." His eyes gleamed with malice. "And I keep what's mine."

The more certain J.T. was that he had her trapped, that she was wasting her time defying him, the more angry Joanna became. He was in for a big surprise if he laid even a pinky finger on her. The woman she'd become was a different person from the one J.T. had first met. This Joanna would never allow herself to be beaten and bullied. This Joanna would fight for herself with all her might.

Joanna choked back a sob of despair at the realization that, however much she kicked and bit and scratched, she had no hope of winning. J.T. was too big. Too strong. And, she knew from experience, injuring him would only make him more vicious when he finally subdued her.

Joanna was sorry now that she hadn't insisted that Harry meet her at the garage. He'd simply left the key in her repaired truck for her to find, willing to wait for payment until after the holiday. There was no one to hear her if she yelled for help. Her screams would be lost among the empty buildings that bordered the garage.

So far, J.T. hadn't tried to grab her. He hadn't even touched her. But he was plainly relishing the terror in her eyes, plainly rejoicing in how wobbly she was on her feet.

Joanna glanced around the parking area, which was concealed from the street, and realized that no one was going to come to her rescue. She was going to have to save herself. If she could somehow get inside the cab of her grandfather's pickup and lock the doors, she could wait for help to come. Even if J.T. broke the windows, it would be hard to drag her out of there. She might be able to use the horn to draw attention to her desperate situation. And if she could hold out for a while inside the cab of the pickup, she was absolutely certain that, sooner or later, Mike would come looking for her.

She just had to distract J.T. long enough to open the passenger door to her grandfather's ancient pickup, which had a tendency to stick, get inside, and punch the locks.

Joanna bared her teeth and said, "That so-called 'ugly' man is a better lover than you could ever be!" then yanked hard on the door to the ancient Dodge.

It was stuck tight.

J.T. stood frozen with outrage for an instant, but the slur seemed to galvanize him, and he jerked her backward. Joanna screamed with fear and frustration as he tore her hands away from the door handle. Somehow, the trunk lid of his Lexus popped open, and Joanna realized that, in a matter of moments, she would be shoved inside. If J.T. got her into that trunk, all was lost.

Mike wouldn't know where to look for her. She'd never told him J.T.'s full name. And Joanna had been too ashamed to tell her grandfather much about the man who'd hit her. Texas was a big place. Mike might never find her. Daisy would think she'd abandoned her.

The thought of being separated from her daughter gave Joanna strength she didn't know she had. She braced her feet against the Lexus bumper, lunging backward to knock J.T. off his feet.

"Oh, no, you don't!" he muttered, lurching sideways but not falling.

She sank her teeth into his exposed wrist where it was wrapped around her chest and bit down hard.

"Ow! You bitch!"

She saw stars when he socked her in the temple, but she didn't let go. J.T. struck her again, this time in her kidney. She thought she would faint and sagged in his arms. He took advantage of the moment to lift her legs into the trunk.

Because her life depended on it, Joanna ignored the pain, arching her body and pushing herself back out, using her fingernails to reach back and tear at J.T.'s face. He shoved her away, grunting as her sharp nails dug deep into his flesh.

Suddenly, J.T. was gone, and her rear end hit the cold, hard ground. She sat stunned for a moment, unable to comprehend what had happened. She heard two male voices snarling at one another, sounds of scuffling, flesh hitting flesh, cries of fury and pain.

Joanna clambered to her feet. Someone had come to her rescue. Tears of joy and relief filled her eyes, blurring her vision. She swiped at them until she could see who it was.

Mike! What had brought him to town? She'd told him he didn't need to come. But he'd come anyway. She'd never been so glad to see his scarred face, which looked truly ferocious distorted by rage and hate.

Mike's fists pummeled J.T.'s ribs and stomach, breaching J.T's pitiful defenses as he hunched his body to protect it from Mike's powerful blows.

Joanna was afraid to say anything, afraid to distract Mike. She wanted to urge him on, urge him to hit and keep on hitting until he'd battered J.T. into mush. But she knew J.T. had the ability to retaliate against Mike in ways that would financially strangle his family's ranch.

So she yelled, "Mike! That's enough!"

Mike glanced at her, then drew back his fist and walloped J.T.'s unprotected jaw. The Texan dropped like a rock on the snowy pavement. He lay there unmoving, defeated so easily by Mike that Joanna could hardly believe it.

Joanna ran to Mike, throwing herself into his waiting arms, pressing herself as close as she could get, sobbing so hard with relief that she couldn't catch her breath.

"Hey," he murmured as his arms folded around her. And then a husky, worried, "Are you all right?"

When he tried to ease her back to look at the bruise she could feel growing on her cheek, she clutched him around the neck and said, "Don't let go."

She was holding on so tight, she wasn't giving him much choice, so he simply picked her up and headed toward his truck. He set her gently in the passenger's seat, before slipping in on the driver's side. She was shivering so hard her teeth were clacking, so he cranked up his pickup and blasted the heater on high.

But Joanna was cold on the inside, where the warmth from the heater couldn't reach. Now that J.T. had found her, she would never be safe in Whitefish. She and Daisy would have to leave Mike and start running again.

Chapter 19

Despite Joanna's pleas to simply drive away, Mike insisted on calling a deputy sheriff who was a friend of the family. Mike promised he'd wait around until the deputy could get there to make sure Joanna's attacker didn't get away.

"Let's just go," Joanna said for the umpteenth time.

"J.T. hit you. He tried to kidnap you. He should be in jail." Mike's knuckles, and his cheekbone where J.T. had gotten in a lucky punch, were raw with pain, and his whole body was still surging with adrenaline. Sitting across the bench seat from him, her arms folded around her shivering body, Joanna was too far away. He should have kept her in his arms. He could already feel the distance growing between them.

"You're wasting your time," Joanna said. "J.T. will post bail and be out in a few hours."

"You're forgetting something."

"What?"

"It's Christmas Eve. There won't be a judge around to let him out for at least forty-eight hours."

"That'll just make him madder."

"So long as he's free, he's a threat to you," Mike said.

"I know." She shot him a look that as good as said, "Now that he's found me, I can't stay here."

Mike grimaced, not caring how bad it made him look. "So you're going to run again? Pack up and leave Whitefish?" *Remove yourself and Daisy from my life?* His heart clutched. "Don't do it."

"What choice do I have?"

"Stay here. Marry me."

She had the sweetest, saddest smile on her face he'd ever seen. "I would love to stay. I would love to marry you someday. But I can't. J.T. would ruin you and your family financially just for spite."

"He might be a lot less able to hurt us than you think."

"He's rich and—" Joanna began.

"His money won't help him."

"You don't understand. J.T.'s connected to everyone who's anyone in Texas."

"Won't make a bit of difference," Mike countered. "Rye's biological father, Angus Flynn, is one of the richest men in the country. Five years ago he married my mother and became my stepfather. I think he can handle that lump of trash I left bleeding on the pavement."

Joanna's brows rose in astonishment. "But you live—"

"In a cabin and work as a rancher," Mike finished for her. "Money doesn't mean a lot to my family. We're happy with our lives the way they are."

At that moment, the deputy arrived. Mike spoke to him through the truck window, briefly explaining what had happened, then began backing out of Harry's parking lot.

He noticed that Joanna's gaze remained focused on J.T. as the deputy cuffed the Texan's hands behind his back where he lay on the snowy pavement and then hauled him to his feet.

She turned to Mike and said in an awed voice, "He's really going to jail."

"For a couple of days, anyway," Mike said as he pulled onto the street and headed toward the ranch. "This arrest will be on J.T.'s record, and if we both testify in court, he may face some legal consequences. But I think I'll let Angus make it clear to J.T. that if he comes anywhere near you again he'll be the one facing financial disaster."

Joanna scooted across the bench seat and leaned her head against Mike's shoulder. He slid his arm around her and said, "It sounded for a moment there like you might be willing to marry me if you weren't being hounded by a madman."

"I was. I am."

Mike yanked his pickup to the curb and shoved it into park. He took both her hands in his and said, "Joanna Henderson, I love you. Will you marry me?"

She laughed and said breathlessly, "This is crazy! You barely know me."

"I know everything I need to know. I want to spend my life with you."

She put a hand on his chest, over his heart, which was beating hard. With hope. And with fear. Joanna had said she might be willing to marry him "someday." It seemed to him that she was using the brief amount of time they'd known each other as a reason to put him off. He wondered if that was the real reason for her hesitation. Or whether it was the one thing about himself that he couldn't change.

"Oh, Mike," she said, her eyes searching his, her hand leaving his chest to graze his scarred cheek, as though to deny that his ruined face made any difference. "This is so sudden. There's so much we haven't discussed."

"Like what?" He heard the harshness in his voice. The rising dread that she was looking for excuses. The panicked feeling that, free of J.T., she would spread her wings and fly . . . away from him.

She seemed to struggle for words and finally said, "I don't know, exactly. Maybe what our life together might look like."

"I'll support whatever you want to do."

Joanna shook her head and crinkled her nose in apparent disbelief. "You say that now. What happens when we disagree?"

"We'll compromise," he said promptly.

"That hasn't been my experience with men in the past."

"You weren't with me in the past," he argued. "Look, Joanna, I can't promise we won't argue. I'm sure we will. But I'll always listen to you and try my best to make you happy."

She didn't say anything for a moment. He hoped that meant she was considering the possibility of a life spent being loved by—and loving—him.

Finally she said, "There must be something you want from me if we get married."

If we get married. That suggested she was actually considering his proposal.

Mike's heart felt like it was trying to escape his chest. He had the feeling that her decision might depend in no small part on what he said next. He knew he should stop and think and choose his words carefully. Instead, he blurted, "Your love. That's all I want. If you love me, all things are possible."

Joanna lowered her gaze to her hands, which were threaded together in her lap, so he couldn't see what she was thinking. She was quiet so long his stomach had a chance to tie itself into excruciating knots that rivaled the painful one growing in his throat. He could hear his aching heart thudding in his chest.

He was afraid to move, afraid to breathe.

When she looked up again, he knew from the joy in her eyes what his answer would be. She said the words anyway.

"Yes, I'll marry you."

Mike gave a whoop of joy and whisked her onto his lap. He felt her happiness as he covered her mouth with his, giving sustenance to the woman he loved and taking it in return.

She broke the kiss long enough to catch his damaged face between her hands and say, "I love you, Mike."

She didn't need to say it twice. Mike's mouth captured hers again, and they might have stayed there the rest of the day, except he remembered there was one more person who had to agree to this marriage.

He tore his lips away and said, "We need to talk to Daisy."

"She loves you, too, Mike."

"I just want to hear from her that it's okay for me to be her dad."

Chapter 20

A herd of horses galloped through Joanna's stomach as she considered how her life was about to change. She glanced across the church pew at the man who would become her husband. She could hardly believe the events of the day. She was glad and nervous and excited. And very, very happy.

Daisy was sitting on Mike's lap, carefully holding a lighted candle with a circular paper at the base to protect her from hot melting wax. Joanna angled the hymnal so Mike could see the words as they sang the third verse of *Joy to the World*, the song that concluded the Christmas Eve program.

They'd decided to wait until they got home after the candlelight service to talk with Daisy about J.T.'s arrest and their decision to marry. Joanna wasn't sure how Daisy would react to the news about J.T., whether she would be glad or sad or scared. As far as their engagement went, Joanna didn't think Daisy could keep that a secret once she knew about it, and

Joanna and Mike wanted to be the ones to tell his family when they were around the table on Christmas Day.

"Time to blow out the candle, Daisy," Mike said.

Daisy huffed three times before she managed to get the candle out. She turned and grinned at Joanna. "I did it."

"You sure did," Joanna said.

Mike picked Daisy up in his arms as Joanna stood with him to leave.

At that moment, Rye and Vick and their kids came up the aisle from the front of the church, noisily greeting Joanna, Mike, and Daisy. Rye and Vick's children had participated in the manger scene at the altar and were still dressed variously as a wise man, a shepherd, and angels. Rye stayed back after his four kids had raced down the aisle toward the door, dragging Vick along with them, and said, "The deputy called and told us what J.T. did to you this morning, Joanna. I just wanted to say I'm glad he's in jail where he belongs. See you guys tomorrow. Merry Christmas!"

Joanna's glance shot toward her daughter at the mention of J.T.'s name. Daisy had clutched Mike around the neck and was staring at Joanna with a look of fright.

"I told you J.T. was here," Daisy wailed, "but you didn't believe me!" She reached out to touch the bruise Joanna had tried to hide with makeup. "Did he hit you again, Mommy?" Without waiting for an answer, Daisy started to cry.

Joanna exchanged a worried look with Mike and said, "Let's sit back down for a minute."

The only two people left in church besides them were dropping hymnals into slots behind the benches where they belonged, picking up discarded programs, and collecting used candles that hadn't been left in the box at the back of the church, preparing for the Christmas morning service. Joanna waited until the last echoes of their activity faded and the hallowed space was silent except for Daisy's sobs. The church that had felt so warm and welcoming and joyful when they'd arrived, suddenly felt cold and dark and oppressive.

Daisy lifted her head from Mike's shoulder, her face tear-drenched, and asked, "Did J.T. come to take you away?"

Joanna nodded, because her throat was too swollen with emotion to speak.

"Do I have to go to board school now?"

"No, sweetheart. No," Joanna said, shaking her head to reinforce her words.

At the same moment, Mike said, "Never, sweetie. Never."

Daisy's gaze shifted from one adult to the other. "But if J.T.'s here—"

"You don't have to worry about him. He's in jail," Mike said.

Daisy looked puzzled, rather than reassured.

"She doesn't know what jail is," Joanna explained to Mike. She turned to Daisy and said, "J.T. can't hurt us anymore."

"J.T. told me he can take what he wants, and no one can stop him," Daisy retorted.

"Mike did." Joanna said. "When J.T. tried to take me away, Mike made him let me go."

Daisy looked up at Mike in awe. "You did?"

Mike nodded. "I'm really strong." Mike made a muscle and said, "Feel this."

Daisy reached out tentatively and felt Mike's muscle. She turned back to Joanna and asked, "J.T.'s really gone?"

"He's really gone," Joanna confirmed.

"We don't have to run away anymore?"

"We never have to run or hide again," Joanna said. "We're staying right here. With Mike."

"I promise I'll always keep you and your mom safe," Mike said, smoothing his hand over Daisy's head.

Daisy slid off his lap onto the floor and turned to look him in the eye. "For how long?"

Mike said, "I think your mom needs to answer that question."

Daisy focused her gaze on Joanna, who said softly, "Forever and ever."

It took Daisy a moment to work out what Joanna had said. She turned back to Mike and asked, "Are we going to live in your house and never leave?"

Mike grinned. "Yep."

"What if J.T. comes back?" Daisy asked.

"I won't ever let him take you or your mommy away. You're going to be my little girl." He hesitated, then added, "If that's all right with you."

"Yes!" Daisy said, climbing back onto Mike's lap, grabbing him around the neck, and hiding her nose against his throat. "And you and me and Mommy will always be together?"

Mike met Joanna's gaze with eyes that brimmed with tears, reached for her hand, and pulled it close to his heart.

"The three of us together. Always and forever."

Epilogue

Mike lay in bed with his arm around his very pregnant wife. He was in no hurry to get up. Snow crystals spattered against the windowpane, while blustery winds rustled through the trees. Christmas had come again. Along with a blizzard. As the sky lightened, he knew it wouldn't be long before Daisy woke up and raced to the living room to see what presents Santa had left under the tree. He heard the soft patter of his daughter's stocking feet on the hall floor and then a screech that could have raised the rafters.

He smiled when he heard her yell, "Daddy! Come see! Santa got my letter. I have a red bike with streamers on the handlebars."

Being called "Daddy" was new, and he was still getting used to it. But he liked it. He liked it a lot.

Daisy had explained at the breakfast table a few days ago that she needed to stop calling him "Mike" and start calling him "Daddy" so the new baby would know the right word to use. "What do you think?" she'd asked, her eyes hopeful and, all these months later, still not quite believing the depth of the love he showered on her.

"Good idea," he'd said past the lump in his throat.

The memory of his daughter's radiant smile as he'd replied made Mike's eyes brim with tears. Lately, his emotions rose fast and hit him hard. Rye joked that Mike was acting like the one in the family with too many hormones. Mike had been a nervous wreck over the past eight and a half months, but he couldn't help it. Joanna had often reached out to smooth the perpetual wrinkles on his scarred brow.

Mike blinked the tears away because he didn't want them to be the first thing Joanna saw when she woke up. He didn't want her thinking he was worrying—yet again—about her, and he would have felt foolish explaining the real reason he was crying. Mike nudged his precious wife's shoulder with his bearded chin and said, "Are you awake?"

"I am now," she said, turning onto her back, shoving the covers away, and groaning as she stretched her arms up and her toes down.

Mike had never stopped marveling at Joanna's pregnant belly. He couldn't resist touching, knowing their child was growing inside her. "How are you feeling?" he asked.

"Like a beached whale."

He knew that was supposed to be funny, and he made himself chuckle. But the closer Joanna got to term, the less amusing he found anything regarding her pregnancy.

Mike didn't see how her skin could keep stretching to accommodate what was turning out to be a very large baby for even another day, let alone another two weeks. He laid his hand on her belly and felt what he thought might be a foot thump against his hand.

"She's been rowdy all night," Joanna said. "I didn't get a wink of sleep."

Since Joanna had been snoring for the past half hour, that wasn't precisely true. But Mike had felt her changing position often, trying to get comfortable, which she'd already told him was impossible lately. On their way home from the Christmas Eve candlelight service, she'd complained that her back was "aching." By bedtime, she'd amended that to "killing me." He'd done his best—which wasn't enough—to massage away the pain, pressing his thumbs into the spots she indicated and amazed when she kept saying, "Harder."

Despite being an anxious prospective father, Mike was almost as excited about having another daughter as Daisy was about having a sister. He wasn't sure how he felt about knowing the sex of their child in advance. The good thing was they'd been able to choose a name.

Daisy had wanted to name her sister Rose. "So she can be a flower, like me."

Joanna had suggested Diana. "I've always liked the Roman myth about Diana the Huntress, goddess of the woods and wild animals, which seems appropriate, considering where we live and what happened to you. And both girls would have names starting with the letter D."

"Winter," Mike had blurted.

Joanna had cocked her head, apparently perplexed at his choice. "Because . . .?"

"Winter is what brought us together," he'd explained,

his cheeks ruddy with embarrassment at the sentimental suggestion. "If it hadn't been for that blizzard, we would never have met."

"I like winter," Daisy said, "'cause the snow is so pretty. And Christmas comes in winter, which is the best time of all."

Joanna's hands took a prayerful pose under her chin as she considered Mike's choice. "Winter Sullivan. Winter Diana Sullivan. Winter Diana Rose Sullivan," she murmured. Her blue eyes suddenly crinkled and her dimples appeared. "Perfect. I love it!"

Mike confessed, "This may be the first time in my life I've looked forward to seeing a Winter in Montana."

"What? You don't like frozen pipes, shoveling twelve feet of snow, and gale-force winds trying to blow the house down?" Joanna asked with mock astonishment.

Mike laid a hand across his heart. "I promise to love Winter for the rest of my life."

Joanna had laughed. Daisy had clapped her hands. Mike's stomach had turned dizzying somersaults. Giving their child a name had made her, and the dangers of Joanna's pregnancy, more real.

He consoled himself with the thought that Joanna had been seeing a doctor regularly and would have the best of care at the Kalispell Regional Medical Center when she delivered the baby. But he'd seen an accident on U.S. 93, the main route from Whitefish to Kalispell, back up traffic for hours. And if the weather was bad, like it was today, they might have trouble getting to the hospital at all.

Mike would have been happy to take a hotel room in

Kalispell for the last month of Joanna's pregnancy, but she'd argued that leaving home wouldn't be fair to Daisy, who searched the house every morning for her elf and looked forward to Santa putting presents under the Christmas tree they'd decorated together.

"Mommy! Daddy! Come open your presents," Daisy yelled.

Mike sat up, rubbed his tired eyes—he'd woken up every time Joanna moved—and said, "We better get up."

"Mike."

He knew the instant Joanna said his name that there was a problem. He shoved the covers the rest of the way off and said, "What's wrong?"

"There's blood on the sheets."

One look at Joanna's face told him that couldn't be good. "Do you feel well enough to dress yourself?" he asked. "Or do I need to help you?"

In answer, she shifted her feet over the edge of the bed and headed for the bathroom down the hall.

"Daisy!" Mike called as he stuck his legs into a pair of Levi's. "Come here."

"Aren't we going to open presents?" she called back.

"Daisy Sullivan, get your butt in here," Mike shouted. "Now!" The adoption wasn't final yet, but Daisy *Sullivan* was already more his daughter than legal papers could ever make her.

He heard silence and then the pounding of feet. Daisy arrived at the bedroom door, her face awash with the kind of fear he hadn't seen in months.

Mike realized it was the first time he'd raised his voice

to her. "I'm not mad at you," he reassured her as he pulled on a University of Montana sweatshirt. "I'm sorry I yelled, but Mommy needs to go to the hospital *right now*, so you need to get dressed as quick as you can."

He saw the tension in her tiny shoulders ease as she asked, "Is the baby coming?"

Mike didn't know, but he didn't want to worry her, so he said, "I think so."

Daisy yelled, "I gotta get dressed!" and ran for her bedroom.

Mike hurried down the hall, rapped his knuckles softly on the bathroom door and said, "Are you all right in there?"

Joanna opened the door, her eyes filled with relief and alight with excitement. "My water broke!"

Mike had read so much literature about pregnancy to educate himself that he actually knew what that meant. "So that bit of blood on the sheets—"

"Means it's time for our little girl to be born," she finished with a brilliant smile. "I'll call the doctor and give her a heads-up."

Mike fought back a spurt of panic. He wasn't ready. This was too soon. It was Christmas Day, for heaven's sake! *And there's a fierce blizzard raging outside.* Panic reared its head again and left him shaken. "We need to get moving," he said to Joanna. "Do you need help dressing?"

She put a soothing hand on his scarred cheek. "Darling, I'm fine."

He saw a startled look in her eyes before she circled her enormous belly with both hands and stood perfectly still. "Oh. That was a lot stronger than the first contraction I had with Daisy."

"So you're definitely in labor?" he said.

"Looks that way," she replied as she walked past him down the hall to their bedroom.

Mike knew Joanna experienced no pain between contractions, but he didn't see how she could be so *calm*. "Daisy, are you ready to go?" Mike called as he headed past her door.

Daisy stepped into the hall dressed in the sort of coveralls his nieces always wore and carrying two dolls—she'd never given up the one with the broken face. "Is it time?"

"Not quite yet. You can play in your bedroom till your mom's ready," Mike said.

"Okay," Daisy said.

Mike continued down the hall to his bedroom, where he found Joanna dressed in a Baylor University sweatshirt that bulged over a pair of maternity jeans. She was standing beside the chest of drawers holding cowboy boots in one hand and a pair of socks in the other. "I need some help getting my socks on."

She froze in place, and he saw that strange look appear in her eyes again. She dropped both socks and boots to grab her belly.

"Another contraction?" he said. "So soon? I thought they were supposed to be thirty minutes apart when they first start."

Joanna gasped. "That one was much, much stronger."

Mike saw confusion and fear in her eyes.

"Something's not right," she said. "The contractions are really strong, and they're a lot closer together than they should be at the beginning of labor."

Then Mike remembered something else he'd read. "Oh, God. I think I know what's going on here. I read about it in one of those childbirth books."

"What are you talking about?" Joanna said.

"All last night, you must have been having *back* labor. Your body does all the same work, but you feel the pain in your back, not across your belly. You started complaining about your back hurting right after church. That means you've probably been in labor for at least ten hours."

Joanna bent over as another contraction hit, and she stayed that way for thirty-seven seconds. Mike knew how long it was because he timed it.

Joanna finally stood upright and said. "That one was really bad. I'm sorry, Mike."

"Sorry? About what?"

She glanced out the bedroom window at the violent snowstorm. "I don't think we're going to make it to the hospital in Kalispell."

"Whitefish is closer. We'll go there."

Joanna bit her lower lip and shook her head. "My contractions are too long and too close together."

"What are you saying?" Mike asked, his heart in his throat.

"You're going to have to deliver this baby."

"That's crazy!" Mike said. "I don't have the first clue—"

"You've delivered plenty of calves," she interrupted. "It can't be that different."

"You're a human, not a cow," Mike retorted.

Joanna began panting. When the contraction ended,

she exhaled a shuddering breath and said, "You can do this, Mike. I trust you."

Mike had never heard sweeter words in a more frightening situation. He shoved a hand through his hair, leaving it askew. "Shouldn't we call the doctor again?" Mike asked, hearing the fear in his voice.

"I'll let her know to stand by the phone, in case we need help," Joanna said.

Mike suddenly realized that Daisy was standing in their bedroom doorway looking distressed.

"Is Mommy gonna be okay?"

"She'll be fine." Mike went down on one knee and took Daisy by the shoulders. "We're not going to the hospital, sweetie. The weather's too bad, and the baby's coming too soon for us to get there in time. So I need your help. Can you get me some string and a pair of scissors from the kitchen? You know which drawer they're in, right?"

"Uh-huh. Should I get them now?"

"Right now," Mike replied.

Daisy turned and bolted down the hall.

"Don't run with the scissors!" he yelled after her.

The instant she was out of sight, Mike ripped off the sheets and got clean ones from the linen closet. He was halfway done remaking the bed when Joanna said, "Can you get my nightgown from the suitcase I was going to take to the hospital?"

He rummaged around and found it, but when he held it out to her, she clutched the bedpost with both hands and screamed in agony. When the contraction was over, she met his gaze, huffed out a breath, and said, "I'll take that nightgown now."

Daisy stood white-faced in the bedroom doorway, a pair of scissors in one hand and a ball of white string in the other. When Mike took them from her she focused her gaze on Joanna and said in a tremulous voice, "Mommy?"

"I'm okay, sweetheart," Joanna said. "This part of having a baby is called labor because it's very hard work."

"You were making a lot of noise," Daisy said.

"I'll probably make a lot more," Joanna replied with a hard-won smile that turned Mike's stomach upside-down. "But soon you'll have a baby sister to hold and love."

Mike was already anxious enough about delivering a baby for the first time without worrying that Daisy might be upset by something she saw or heard if she stayed in the room. So he suggested, "Why don't you go separate all those Christmas presents into stacks, one for you and one for Mommy and one for me. As soon as your sister is born, we can open them."

Mike gave her a gentle shove and closed the bedroom door. He waited a moment to see whether Daisy would pound on it, wanting to be let back in. He was relieved to hear the faint sound of her feet padding toward the living room.

When he turned back around, Joanna was dressed in the flannel gown she'd planned to take to the hospital. Mike hurried to finish making the bed, then sterilized the scissors with bourbon he kept in a flask in his sock drawer, wet several washcloths with hot water, and found a soft pillowcase in which to wrap the baby. He was as ready as he knew how to be.

Meanwhile, Joanna was having a series of contractions that he could tell by her grunts and groans and stifled screams were agonizing.

He wanted to help, but he didn't know how. The labor that had seemed to be moving so fast now seemed to be taking forever. His own body tensed every time Joanna had an excruciating contraction. He finally asked, "Do you want to sit somewhere or lie down on the bed?"

"I'm better off on my feet," she said through gritted teeth.

She was pacing the bedroom like a wild animal in a cage. A moment later, she glared at him and yelled, "Shit, shit, shit! This is all your fault, you son of a bitch. Damn, that hurts!"

Mike was shocked at Joanna's outburst. She *never* used that sort of language. But sending a baby down the birth canal without anesthesia was obviously no picnic.

Then she said, "I have to push." She stood in one place, grunting for a moment.

When she stopped, Mike scooped her up. "You can do your pushing on the bed lying down. I don't want to be picking our kid up off the floor."

Despite everything, Joanna laughed. "I'm imagining how our family and friends would react to a story like that."

"It's not funny, Joanna." Mike was terrified, wondering if the baby would tear her apart as it forced its way out of her body and into the world. What if she started bleeding, and it didn't stop? Could he get her to the doctor in time to save her life?

He comforted himself with the thought that women had been having babies at home for eons. And tried not to think about how many of them had died.

"I have to push again." Joanna had pulled her nightgown up to her waist, and her knees spread wider as a harsh, grating sound issued from her throat.

"I see the baby's head," he said. "Her hair is black, like mine," he added in a surprised voice.

Joanna lay panting for endless moments, then said, "I have to *puuuuuussssssshhh!*"

Mike was surprised at how easily his wailing daughter slid into his waiting hands. He felt the tears blur his eyes as he looked down at their beautiful little girl.

"She's perfect," he told Joanna. He laid the crying baby on Joanna's stomach while he tied the cord with the string he'd gotten from Daisy and cut it. Then he wrapped Winter Diana Rose Sullivan snugly in a pillowcase and placed her in Joanna's waiting arms.

The baby quieted as Joanna cooed to her, and a short while later, Mike caught the afterbirth in a piece of the newspaper that he'd been reading the night before, wrapped it up, and set it aside, before wiping away what little blood there was on Joanna with a warm washcloth.

Mike sat down beside Joanna and leaned over to kiss her gently on the lips. "How are you feeling?"

"Wonderful."

The door opened and Daisy stuck her head in. "I heard a baby crying."

"Come meet your sister," Joanna said with a warm smile.

Daisy came running, and Mike caught her and lifted her onto the bed between himself and Joanna.

Daisy's blue eyes were wide with awe. "She's so tiny."

Mike thought so too, but Joanna said, "She's bigger than you were."

"Can I hold her?" Daisy asked in a whisper.

"Of course," Joanna said. She lifted their newborn daughter into Daisy's lap and showed Daisy how to support the baby's head.

Mike's heart felt so full it made his chest ache.

Daisy reached out to trace the baby's tiny eyebrow, and Winter's waving hand grasped Daisy's finger. "She likes me!" Daisy said, grinning first at Joanna and then at Mike. Daisy leaned over, kissed her sister on the forehead, and said, "I like you, too, Winter."

Mike hadn't taken an easy breath since Joanna had gone into labor. It dawned on him that Joanna was fine. Daisy was happy. And he was a father for the second time. The gaggle of geese that had been flying around in his stomach finally landed.

I have two wonderful daughters and a wife who loves me. What more, he wondered, *could any man ask of life?*

"Daddy," Daisy said, as Joanna took Winter back into her arms. "I think it's time to open our presents."

"I think you're right, sweetie."

But Mike was certain there was nothing under the Christmas tree that could match the priceless gifts he'd already been given.

LETTER TO READERS

Dear Reader,

Mike's story began, along with the bear attack that mutilated his face, in the fourth book of my King's Brats series, *Sullivan's Promise*. Or, if you're feeling adventuresome, you may want to start at the beginning of my King's Brat series of Bitter Creek novels and read all four books: *Sinful, Shameless, Surrender,* and *Sullivan's Promise*. I've written more than thirty-five contemporary, Regency, and Western Bitter Creek novels. You can find a complete booklist of all sixty-three of my novels and novellas on my website, www.joanjohnston.com. Enjoy!

I'd love to hear from you. You can reach me at my website or find me at instagram.com/joanjohnstonwrites, facebook.com/joanjohnstonauthor, or twitter@joanjohnston.

Happy reading,
Joan Johnston

Introducing

Tales of Modern-day Royalty
by
JOAN JOHNSTON

The Benedict Brothers

Isabella Wharton Benedict, the modern-day
Duchess of Blackthorne, has a dying wish:
to find spouses for her grown children,
four gentlemen rogues and a spoiled rotten lady,
scattered around the world
like a handful of precious jewels.

Continue reading for a peek at two Benedict Brothers novels.

Invincible

and

Unforgettable

INVINCIBLE

Prologue

How hard could it be to find spouses for her five grown children before she died? Bella supposed it depended on how long it took for her failing heart to give out. No one had ever accused the five Benedict children of being easy to handle. All of them over twenty-five and not one of them ever engaged, let alone married.

That might have something to do with the lives they led as members of British royalty. Bella was actually Isabella Wharton Benedict, Duchess of Blackthorne. She certainly had her work cut out for her finding mates for four British-American lords and a lady. Bella corrected herself. Make that four gentlemen rogues and a spoiled rotten lady.

Could she do it? Did she dare try?

Bella stared out the window from her hospital bed at the University of Virginia Medical Center in Charlottesville, wondering where to start. She ran a brush through her shoulder-length black hair, which was threaded with more silver every day. She might be in the autumn of her life, but here in Virginia it was spring, when love blossomed.

Cardinals flirted in the flowering dogwood trees. Blue, black, and yellow butterflies cavorted in the daffodils. Squirrels chattered at each other and played tag, tails flying. With any luck, her titled offspring would find themselves equally vulnerable to romance during this fertile season.

She threw the engraved silver brush onto the bedside table and turned her attention back to the doctor standing at the foot of her hospital bed. "What's the verdict?"

"You're still at thirty percent heart function."

That was actually good news. At least she hadn't lost function since her last checkup. She could live—for a while, maybe years—with that little heart function. But the point was, her heart was dying, and she was dying along with it.

That's what she got for insisting she could ski down an icy slope in the Alps. She'd survived the blunt force trauma to her heart when she'd lost control and gone over a cliff. But the injury had caused scarring that had resulted in reduced heart function and continuing heart failure.

"How long do I have?" she asked.

"The new meds I gave you should keep you up and running for a while."

"Running?" Bella said with a quirk of her lips.

"Figuratively," the doctor qualified. "You should certainly be exercising regularly to keep what's left of your heart muscle healthy. And take your meds!"

Bella eyed the numerous bottles of pills she needed to keep her heart functioning. She hated depending on all those pills, but they allowed her an almost-normal life. ACE inhibitors. Beta blockers. Aldosterone antagonist drugs. She couldn't begin to name the individual prescriptions. The problem was at some point—in the not-too-distant future—her heart was still going to fail.

"How long do I have?" Bella asked again.

"Can't say," the doctor replied.

"Guess."

The doctor shrugged. "A year for sure. Maybe two. Three if you take care of yourself—and you're lucky. Or you could have a heart attack tomorrow. We just can't predict these things."

Bella shivered. That wasn't much of a future.

"I do have some good news," the doctor said.

"I'll take what I can get."

"We've been making enormous strides in stem cell therapy. Stay alive long enough, and we may be able to rejuvenate that heart of yours with your own stem cells.

"How long is long enough?" Bella asked.

The doctor focused on the medical chart in his hands. "Can't say."

'"And if my heart continues to fail?"

"Heart transplant is a possibility down the line. Unfortunately, it won't be easy finding a heart for you, Bella. B-negative donors aren't thick on the ground."

Bella smiled. Her doctor was young, a prodigy whose bedside manner left a lot to be desired. She appreciated his honesty. Knowing how much—or rather, how little—time she had left allowed her to plan how to use it wisely.

But a year? Two years? Three, if she was lucky? She had even less time than she'd hoped to get her children wed. With so little time, some of those marriages might have to be arranged without her offspring's cooperation. It had to be marriage, she'd decided. Nothing less would do. Her marriage to Bull Benedict had been her salvation.

It had started badly, with blackmail on her side. Her aunt had threatened twenty-nine-year-old billionaire financier Jonathan "Bull" Benedict with charges of statutory rape if he didn't marry destitute seventeen-year-old Isabella Wharton, Duchess of Blackthorne. Bull had sworn he'd hate her forever if she forced him into marriage.

She'd bit her lip and gone along with her aunt's wishes in order to save her hereditary home, Blackthorne Abbey. And to give her unborn child a name. It was only later that Bull questioned whether he was the father of their first child. Only later that he learned Oliver was some other man's son.

Because they were bound by law, they'd been forced to deal with one another's lies. Because they were husband and wife, they'd scratched their bloody way through the tangled thorns of deceit to a love that healed all wounds.

Bella wanted her children bound to someone they could love by vows made before God. She was certain the moral commitment created by the spoken words, words pledging love and faith to each other, would give the young lovers the perseverance necessary to work through any differences that threatened their happiness.

She didn't want her children wandering the world alone after she was gone, believing that love was a false thing. That love couldn't be trusted. That was the lesson she feared they'd learned from the wickedness—the malicious trickery— that had finally torn her marriage apart.

"Of course, Bella, if you do end up with a new heart—

or a rejuvenated one—you'll be good to go for another fifty years," the doctor said, interrupting her thoughts.

"Thanks a lot," Bella said with a wry laugh. She was fifty-two. Reaching a hundred and two sounded pretty ambitious. And lonely, unless she could find a way to win her husband's forgiveness. Bella felt hopeless about any sort of reconciliation with Bull. Especially when she considered how little she could tell him—certainly not the truth—about the event that had caused their bitter separation ten years ago, after twenty-five years of marriage.

They were still legally wed, but it was a marriage in name only. They lived separate lives. Every day for the past ten years, she'd feared Bull would come to her and ask for a divorce. It had never happened. She wondered if he was clinging to a fragile thread of hope, as she was, that someday they would find their way back to each other.

Or whether he simply wanted to preserve his fortune. A fortune which, thanks to an ironclad prenuptial agreement, would only have to be shared with her if they stayed married for twenty-five years. They'd reached that mark a month before their abrupt separation.

Bella sighed inwardly. The chances of "love conquering all" seemed slim, considering how little time she had left. She needed to focus on her children's happiness. When the end came would be soon enough to make peace with Bull.

"When can I get out of her?" she asked.

"Today, if you promise to follow my orders," the doctor replied. "Make sure you exercise, Bella. Take your meds. And avoid stress. Otherwise . . ." He drew a finger across his neck, hung his head sideways and made a dying sound.

Bella grimaced at his antics. Maybe she could get Oliver, Riley, Payne, Max, and Lydia to come to her, instead of having to go to the four corners of the earth to find them. Without revealing her precarious health, of course. Mother's Day was coming up. That would make a good excuse to summon them to The Seasons, the Benedict family estate near Richmond, a former tobacco planation her estranged husband's family had owned since colonial days.

The doctor turned to Bella's personal assistant, a quiet, intelligent, almost homely girl Bella had hired three years ago when she first began taking medication for her ailing heart, and ordered, "I don't want her out partying till the wee hours, Emily. Bella needs rest if she's going to stay alive until we can repair her heart—or find her a new one."

"Of course, doctor," Emily replied. "I'll take good care of Her Grace."

Twenty-eight-year-old Emily Sheldon was nothing if not dutiful, Bella thought. The young Englishwoman refused to address Bella by name, instead referring to her in clipped British tones as "Your Grace," an honor to which Bella was entitled by virtue of her aristocratic rank.

The refined, straitlaced young woman, who'd become as dear to her as another daughter, would follow the doctor's orders to the letter. If Bella didn't want to find herself being hounded by her assistant, she was going to have to involve Emily in her matchmaking plans.

When the doctor was gone, Emily began fussing with the sheets, pulling them up around Bella's pale blue silk robe and smoothing them down. "I urge you to consider the consequences if you disobey the doctor's orders, Your Grace. I'll do my best to help you—"

Bella put a hand on her assistant's delicate wrist and said, "Please sit down, Emily. I have something to discuss that's going to require your entire attention—our entire attention—for the foreseeable future."

UNFORGETTABLE

Chapter 1

Lydia felt groggy. She groaned as she stretched out on the luxurious hotel bed. She tried shoving the exquisitely soft Egyptian cotton sheets aside with her feet, but they were tangled in something that felt even more like silk. Which was when Lydia realized she was still wearing her ball gown.

She shoved herself upright and stared down at the wrinkled powder-blue silk, then gasped and put her hands to her throat in search of the priceless pearl necklace she'd worn to last night's masked charity ball at the *Boscolo Exedra Roma*, a magnificent five-star hotel in Rome.

It wasn't there.

The fabulous teardrop-shaped pearl, called the Ghost of Ali Pasha, had been worn over the centuries by sultans and queens, by kings and princesses. It had been given to her mother, Bella, Duchess of Blackthorne, by her father, billionaire banker Jonathan "Bull" Benedict, on the day of Lydia's birth.

Where had it gone?

Lydia's heart began to race, and the copper taste of fear rose in her throat as she frantically searched the bedding for the missing necklace. Perhaps the clasp had come undone. She jumped out of bed and teetered dizzily. She grabbed her head and groaned again. How many lemon drop martinis had she drunk last night?

She could only remember having two. So why was she feeling so dizzy and sick to her stomach? Why had she fallen asleep in her dress? And where, oh where, had she put the Ghost of Ali Pasha?

"Mother's going to kill me!" Especially since Lydia hadn't gotten permission to borrow the necklace in the first place.

She stumbled over her strappy heels, which lay on the floor beside the bed, and accidentally knocked everything off the end table. She dropped to her knees and desperately picked through the debris.

A crumpled Kleenex. A bottle of Delicious Red fingernail polish. She remembered chipping a fingernail and needing to repair it last night before the ball. The room key card. Her Kate Spade clutch purse, which was barely big enough for a few hundred euros, a tube of Raving Red lipstick and her iPhone.

No necklace.

She struggled to her feet and stumbled barefoot to the bathroom, tossing cosmetics around on the dressing table. Her head pounded at the clatter of glass against marble. The lingering, musky smell of Paloma Picasso perfume made her nauseous. She found a pair of diamond earrings and an emerald bracelet, but no pearl necklace.

She staggered out into the sitting room of her elegant suite on the Piazza Trinita dei Monti, at the top of the Spanish Steps, holding on to the antique furniture as she went, her gaze leaping from surface to surface. She threw the flowered pillows off the sofa, then yanked off the cushions to see if the necklace might have fallen behind or beneath them.

Nothing.

Lydia's moan became a wail of despair. How could she have been so careless? Her eldest brother, Oliver, Earl of Courtland, had arranged for her to receive the necklace from the vault at Blackthorne Abbey near London where her mother's precious jewels were stored. She'd promised him that the priceless necklace would be kept in the Hotel Hassler safe every moment it wasn't around her neck.

How was she going to explain her actions to her mother—and to Oliver, who'd trusted her to act responsibly—if she couldn't find the Ghost? She knew for a fact that her father had spent $25 million on the precious jewels—diamonds, rubies, sapphires, and emeralds—that provided a frame for the enormous, irreplaceable teardrop pearl that was the centerpiece of the necklace.

She'd received $50 million in a trust fund this past year when she'd turned twenty-five, but she'd invested the money with the Castle Foundation, founded by her four older brothers to do good works. All she had left was a quarterly allowance. How would she ever make amends for the loss?

Oliver had told her that if she could get permission from their mother to borrow the Ghost, he would make the necessary arrangements to get the necklace to Rome. Lydia had been so sure the duchess would say "No" that she'd never asked. She'd simply told Oliver she had permission. And he'd believed her.

She could never have imagined the disaster that had occurred. Never imagined that the necklace would disappear from around her neck without a trace. Lydia groaned like a dying animal. She idolized her eldest brother. Oliver was going to hate her. Far worse, he was never going to trust her again.

Lydia turned in a circle in the elegant sitting room, with its marble arches and panoramic views of the Eternal City visible through the tall, brocade-curtained windows. "Where is it?" she cried. "Where could it be?"

She felt a sudden burst of hope as a thought came to mind. Maybe she'd dropped the necklace off at the hotel safe on the way up to her room. That made perfect sense. She grabbed the phone and called the front desk. A glance at the sun shining in from the balcony through the open curtains told her it must be almost noon. She never slept that late. How much *had* she drunk?

She remembered having a wonderful time at the masked ball, especially since her mask and costume allowed her to elude the titled gentleman her father wanted her to marry. There was nothing essentially wrong with Harold Delaford, Earl of Sumpter, son and heir of the Marquess of Tenby. He was nice. He practically doted on her. And he was determinedly courting her.

But kissing Harold was like kissing a leather-bound book. There was simply no thrill. There had been no challenge in making Harold—he disliked being called Harry—fall in love with her. He'd been besotted at first glance, as so many men were. Lydia couldn't help the fact that she'd been genetically blessed with both beauty and brains. She had her mother's violet eyes, ivory complexion, and lush figure and her father's black hair, strong chin, and mathematical genius. She had the added bonus of being British royalty as Lady Lydia, daughter of the Duchess of Blackthorne. Lord Delaford expected her to be seen on his arm, but not heard, like some fragile Victorian doll, kept on the shelf, admired but not touched.

She wanted more. She didn't know what, exactly. She yearned for passion. For adventure. For a life that was challenging and romantic and full of surprises. Was that so much to ask? She'd spent most of her life in one British or European boarding school after another, since she managed to get herself thrown out on a regular basis for some mischief. But that was the extent of her brushes with bedlam.

She'd been creating her own excitement for the past six months by emulating the work Oliver did. Not that he knew she'd discovered his secret. Oliver spent his spare time discreetly retrieving stolen artifacts and returning them to their rightful owners. He was currently in Argentina seeking a Russian triptych stolen by the Nazis. She was on a similar quest here in Rome but having considerably less success.

"This is Lydia Benedict," she said when the hotel receptionist answered the phone. "Can you check your records to see whether I returned anything to the safe late last night?"

"I'll check for you, Lady Lydia," a voice replied in Italian.

Lydia hadn't even realized she was speaking Italian. That was the problem with being multi-lingual. "Thank you," she said in British-accented English. She'd probably dropped the necklace off before she'd come upstairs. Surely she had. That was why it wasn't around her neck. It was lying in its black velvet box in the hotel safe.

"You last signed for your box at seventeen hundred hours four minutes, my lady."

Lydia sank onto the sofa, losing her balance when she landed on the low, hard frame, rather than the cushions, which she'd tossed onto the floor. She remembered retrieving the necklace from the safe around 5:00 p.m. the previous evening and coming upstairs to dress for the ball. "Is there any chance I might not have signed in when I gave an item to you for safe-keeping?" she asked hopefully.

"No chance at all, Miss Benedict."

"*Grazie,*" she said as she disconnected the phone. "No no no no no no no no," she muttered. "This can't be happening."

But it was. It had.

What was she going to do? She couldn't bear to see the look on her mother's face the next time she saw her, or on Oliver's face at the next quarterly meeting of the Castle Foundation.

What about Mother's feelings when she discovers the Ghost is missing? The Ghost was a love gift from Father. She'll be devastated at its loss.

Sometimes it was difficult to imagine her mother having feelings. Or being in love. The Duchess of Blackthorne was always so cool and composed, even around her children. Especially around her children. Except, as the youngest of five and the only girl, Lydia knew it was all an act. She'd seen her mother weeping bitterly. She'd seen the forlorn look on the duchess's face after one of Bull and Bella's many violent arguments before their separation ten years ago.

Lydia was sure her mother still loved her father.

Otherwise she wouldn't have cried such hopeless tears over their separation. Lydia shuddered when she remembered what had happened when she'd tried to comfort her mother.

It hadn't been easy reaching out to the duchess. She'd always been a distant mother. Lydia had come home to Blackthorne Abby from boarding school in Switzerland for a short vacation and had barely seen her parents during the visit. She'd always yearned to be closer to her mother, and she couldn't help wanting to comfort someone in as much pain as her mother seemed to be.

Lydia had barely laid a hand on her mother's shoulder when the duchess whipped around and confronted her with an angry look. The duchess already had her mouth open to chastise the intruder when she realized it was Lydia. "Oh."

That was all her mother said. Not "I could use a hug" or "Come here, sweetheart" or "Thank you for caring." What she'd finally said was, "I need to be alone."

Alone with her pain. That was how Lydia imagined her mother had lived the past ten years without her father, alone at Blackthorne Abbey, the hereditary castle of the Dukes of Blackthorne in Kent, about an hour south of London. All alone. Except for all the paramours, of course, whose arm would be entwined with hers at whatever social or charity event her parents were inevitably both attending somewhere in the world.

Her father was no better. Equally distant. Equally remote from his children. He spent most of his time at the Paris office of his banking empire. Both parents had flaunted their lovers over the past ten years, creating great tabloid fodder and making Lydia's life at boarding school a nightmare—until she confronted the gossips with acid remarks about their own genealogy. That shut them up. At least until her parents' next flagrant public misbehavior.

Many times Lydia had wished Bella and Bull would just get a divorce and be done with it. The gossips said her father refused to divorce her mother because he would have been forced to split his fortune with her if they did. Lydia didn't for a moment think that was the reason they were still married. It was as obvious as the pain on both their faces that they were still deeply in love with each other. She often wondered what it was that had torn them apart and whether the breach could ever be mended.

Lydia felt her throat clogging with emotion. She was sorry to have lost her mother's necklace, but even more than her mother's censure, she dreaded the consequences Oliver might face for having given her the necklace in the first place. There had to be some way to figure out how and when the Ghost had disappeared.

"Of course!" she said, lurching from the sofa toward the bedroom and the pile of stuff she'd left on the floor beside the bed.

Lydia located her iPhone and punched in a number that connected her with her mother's executive assistant, Emily Sheldon. Emily was in her early thirties, a slender woman with a homely face—that sounded cruel to say, but it was the absolute truth—warm brown eyes, a kind heart and a large, poverty-stricken family she seemed to be single-handedly supporting, both emotionally and financially.

Lydia had to tell someone what had happened. Emily had been Lydia's confidante more than once during the past three years since the young woman had become the duchess's assistant, and never once had she revealed any of the secrets Lydia had shared.

"Emily?" she choked out when the phone was answered. "Lady Lydia? Is that you?" Emily asked.

Lydia struggled to hold back a sob. "I'm in trouble, Emily!"

"Where are you, Lydia? Are you all right? Do you need help?"

Lydia could tell Emily was upset because she'd forgotten the "Lady" she always inserted before "Lydia." Emily was a stickler for the proprieties, even though neither Lydia, nor any of her siblings, cared whether they were addressed by their British titles. "No one can help," Lydia said at last.

"Let me call Lord Oliver—"

"Not Oliver!" Lydia cried. "I don't want him to know what's happened." Not until she had no other choice.

"Calm down," Emily said. "I won't contact Lord Oliver, if you don't want me to. Tell me where you are."

"Rome."

"Are you in danger?"

"Not exactly," Lydia replied.

Emily's British accent was clipped as she asked, "Are you in danger, my lady? Or not?"

Lydia half sobbed, half laughed and said, "Only from Mother. She's going to kill me when she finds out what I've done."

"The duchess loves you, Lady Lydia. There's nothing you can do that she won't forgive."

"Really?" Lydia said. "What do you think she'll say

when she finds out I've lost the Ghost?"

Emily gasped.

There was no other sound from the other end of the line. At last Lydia said, "Emily? Are you still there?"

"What happened?" Emily asked, her voice surprisingly calm.

"I told Oliver I had Mother's permission to borrow the necklace, so he arranged to have it delivered to me in Rome. I wore it to a charity ball last night. Sometime during the night, the Ghost disappeared."

"From the hotel safe?" Emily asked.

"I didn't put it back in the safe."

"Oh, Lady Lydia."

Lydia heard the disapproval in the other woman's voice and said defensively, "When I got back to my hotel—" She realized she didn't know exactly when or even how she'd gotten back to her hotel room. That was a mystery she was going to have to unravel. It seemed safer, more honest, to simply say, "I never returned it to the safe."

"How long has the necklace been missing?"

"I don't know. I just woke up—it's a little after noon here in Rome—and discovered it wasn't around my neck or in the room or in the hotel safe. I couldn't believe it at first. I've been looking everywhere for what seems like hours. It isn't here."

"Please let me call Lord Oliver."

"No! Please, please, Emily. Don't tell Oliver. He thought I had permission to borrow the necklace. He'll get in trouble, too. I don't want him to know I lost it like this. He said I could keep it for ten days. There's another charity event coming up, and he said I could wear it for both. There's still time for me to find the Ghost before I'm supposed to return it. Once I find it, I can apologize to Mother, and to Oliver, for being so careless, but not until then."

Once again, Lydia heard silence on the other end of the line. She didn't know where to turn if Emily couldn't help her. She held her breath waiting for her mother's capable assistant to come up with a solution to her dilemma.

At last Emily said, "I'm going to call someone to come and help you find the necklace. His name is Sam Warren. He's a private investigator from America, from Dallas, Texas, to be precise. He's the very best, Lydia. He should be there by tomorrow morning. Don't worry. If Sam can't find the Ghost, it can't be found.

"But it *has* to be found!"

Emily gave a shaky laugh. "What I meant to say is that Mr. Warren will find it. He's never failed on a mission your mother has given him yet."

"Thank you, thank you, thank you, Emily!" Lydia felt almost giddy with relief. "Let me know when his flight is arriving here in Rome, and I'll go meet it."

"Oh, dear. I don't think Sam will want your help."

"He doesn't have any choice," Lydia said with conviction. "I lost the Ghost. And I intend to be there when it's found."

Made in the USA
Monee, IL
18 April 2020